Southern Grit & Glamour

Back in Thyme

Elizabeth, Sing your song! Marsha Thauwald

WRITTEN BY MARSHA THAUWALD

ILLUSTRATED BY ERIN BROWN

ISBN: 978-1-5356-0759-9

Dedication

Southern Grit& Glamour—Back in Thyme is dedicated in memory of my aunts—Allene, Maurine, Gertie, Faye, Nell, and Charlene. I look forward to seeing you all again when I finally come home to heaven!

Endorsements

Reading this book is like catching up with old friends; it is a sweet and fun continuation of the mystery, adventure, and touch of romance that began in *Big Southern Hair & Highlights*. Readers will enjoy reconnecting with the now grown-up Cora Jean and Cara as they continue to discover new secrets about their family and events of the past. A great story with a beautiful lesson about family, love and forgiveness.

Diane McDaniel
River Valley Intermediate School Librarian and
Booktalk Guru

I thoroughly enjoyed reading "Southern Grit & Glamour!" I loved the colorful descriptions of the sisters that make up the heart of this story. Marsha Thauwald truly captured the spirit and character of what I have come to know and love of the strong, fun-loving & full of faith women of Texas!

Sue Connor
Transplanted Texas Resident

Southern Grit & Glamour is a sweet and heartfelt read. It will make you cry every thyme!

Emma Willson
Age 12

"After reading Big Southern Hair and Highlights, I was curious to know more about CJ and Cara, long lost twin sisters. The sequel brings their lives together and I loved every minute of this intriguing plot. Most readers of all ages would enjoy reading this compelling story of the grown-up twins."

Marianne Lanman
93-year-old Jimmie's granddaughter

"It is not often that I find myself loving a sequel as much as I love *Southern Grit & Glamour*. Once again, Marsha takes her readers into the lives of twin sisters CJ & Cara and their friends and families - sharing their adventures and challenges with twists, turns and intrigue. It is the perfect middle grade book that all children and their families will enjoy. I can only hope that she has a third story in the works!"

Bill Barrett
Senior Vice President Sales & Marketing
Scholastic Book Fairs

"*Southern Grit & Glamour* is a real page turner. Readers will imagine hearing the Southern Grit and Glamour music in their heads as the mystery of Betsy Grace's disappearance unfolds."

Anne Lee
Senior Leader of Independent Reading Advocacy
Scholastic Book Fairs

"I *loved* this book!"   Kimi Smith "Sweet 16"

"This new book by Marsha Thauwald uncovers more about the lives of the extended family of CJ and Cara. The sacrifices that were made to ensure that CJ and Cara had a life full of love and family are more evident as they grow up and become blessings to those around them."

Becca Bell, Braxton's and Cannon's Bebe

PRAISE for *Big Southern Hair & Highlights, Please don't dye without us*
    "*Big Southern Hair & Highlights is a great accomplishment for author Marsha Thauwald. I loved it!!*"

Lauren Tarshis
Author of the <u>*I Survived*</u> Series

Acknowledgements

This segment is probably my favorite. Readers don't relish the words I am about to express, but as the writer, these next words are priceless.

First of all I want to thank my family and friends who were inspirations for the fictional characters in my book or helped me read the manuscript prior to publication.

Ashley, Sam, Emma, and Bethany (Bea) Willson; Jason, Tara, Jet, and Ali Jane Taylor; Pete, Justin, Nathan, Chelsea, Carrington, and Collyns Thauwald; Billye Talley; Leslie and Kimi Smith; Sue Connor; Becca Bell; Bill Barrett; Anne Lee; Marianne Lanman; Michael Phillips; Michael Morrill; Diane McDaniel; Ray Nell Petty; Jailee, Tallulah, Carson, and Judson

Much appreciation to Isaiah Austin, Former Baylor Bear Basketball player and author of *Dream Again*.

Thank you, Adrienne Witzel for your expertise with archeology. Betsy Grace would not have been found without your advice.

A very special thanks to Lauren Tarshis, author of the *I Survived* Series who took the time to read the first book, **Big Southern Hair & Highlights**. I hope she finds the sequel worth the read, too.

Finally, I thank God for giving me the desire to write these stories. I want to remember to praise you for this opportunity every day. It's your day, Lord; it's your day!

Table of Contents

Prologue

"Good things stand like stone: kindness in another's trouble, courage in your own."
Cora Howe Nashville, 1932

The journey began when two little girls were born in Truway, Texas in the heart of Buford County on October 9, 1956. Their mother died mysteriously soon after they were born. One of them stayed in Truway with her great aunt, Lottie Jean Trinity, owner of the Big Southern Hair Beauty Salon. The other one was taken to Las Bonitas Ranch in New Mexico to live with her great aunt, Thelma Louise Tune.

Cora Jean, nicknamed CJ, lived an adventurous life in her hometown and tried to stay out of trouble by hanging out at her aunt's Big Southern Hair Beauty Salon. Her life got even more exciting when she found her mother's diary in their cellar and found out she had a twin sister she didn't know existed.

Cara lived on the Las Bonitas Ranch with her constant companion, Sam, the snow-white burro. She was diagnosed at a young age with Marfan syndrome which affected her eyes and joints. Lottie and Thelma made the decision to separate the twins when they realized Cara needed special care and thought it best for her to be raised alone on the ranch.

CJ and Cara finally get the chance to meet at the age of fourteen when they both enrolled in the Greenwood School for Girls in El Paso. While there, they got the opportunity not only to build their relationship as sisters, but to read their mom's diary. Through Jean's words the girls met their father, Joe Smallwood, a chef at the Whistle Stop Cafe who was tragically killed in a train accident before the girls were born. They found out about Jean's old high school flame, Jas Luke Chilacothe who was from the wealthiest family in Buford County and who rekindled their romance only to lose her to a premature death.

Intrigue surrounded other people in their mom's life like Geraldine Chilacothe, Bernice Jones, and last but not least, John Mark Chilacothe, Geradine's husband and Jas Luke's father. Not only was Brother

Mike from their church a true friend to the family, he was an admirable person who inspired and encouraged others with his words of wisdom. He spent his time teaching the Truway folks what it means to love and forgive.

The journey continued for several decades through adventures in Truway and Las Bonitas Ranch.

Now, the twins are grown and content with their lives until they learn of yet another relative dying mysteriously. They'll have to go back in time to find out what happened. They will travel to an era when their great aunts were growing up and hear about the musical group, ***Southern Grit and Glamour***.

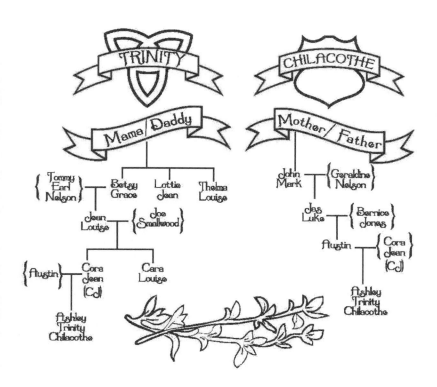

Chapter 1
A Wedding in Truway, Texas (Lottie, 1982)

"My love is true, so true for you."
Lyrics from *My Love is True*

As I sit in my Sunday pew and watch the exchange of wedding vows between CJ and Austin, I can't help thinking about the day that CJ and her twin sister, Cara met. I'll never forget their expressions when they saw each other for the first time, just like I'll never forget the expression shared between CJ and Austin today.

CJ and Cara didn't know the other existed during their formative years. I often ask myself, "Was it right to keep the girls apart for so long?" The answer changes every time I ask the question. I know that CJ will be committed to her sister until the day she dies and Cara will do the same. If only Jean were alive to see one of her daughters get married. CJ looks so much like her mama. Her smile and her mannerisms remind me so much of Jean. I'd never seen her mama with her hair twisted up as fancy as CJ's was today, but they shared the same habit of putting it up and out of the way. CJ stood with her mother's confidence, narrow shoulders back and head held high. The bright grin on her face was nearly identical to the one her mother wore when she was affected with unbearable happiness. I know Jean is smiling down from heaven watching CJ and Cara stand side-by-side.

* * *

My name is Lottie Jean Trinity and I have called Truway, Texas home for sixty-six years. Truway is the home of The Big Southern Hair & Highlights Salon, Jean & Joes' Place, and The Flower Shop. The salon has been around since the 1930's, but the other two establishments have only been here since the '70's. Della's Diner was bought and changed to Jean & Joe's Place in memory of the girls' parents.

I'm proud to say that I own all three of these establishments and until recently managed the salon by myself. There's only one other place older than Big Southern Hair and that's Chilacothe Farms, "Where

Thyme Makes a Difference-"-John Mark Chilacothe, proprietor. "Thyme" is defined as *a low-growing aromatic plant of the mint family. The small leaves are used as a culinary herb.*

Most of us hadn't heard about thyme until John Mark brought some into to town and made an announcement to the local residents about how he was going to add it to his vegetables and sell it to grocers around the state back in the 30's. The idea caught on and now his vegetables with thyme are sold all over the United States.

All of the proprietors in Truway get together every time there's a new birth in town and decide to have some type of special to celebrate. When twins are born, it's a given that there will be a two-for-one deal featured. For example, The Big Southern Hair & Beauty Salon gave a manicure and a pedicure for the price of one when the last twins were born to Mr. Johnson's son and daughter-in-law. Jean and Joe's Place featured their specialty items, Joe's Burrito and Jean's Delight for the price of the burrito, and The Flower Shop gave away a beautiful yellow rose bud for every flower arrangement purchased.

I have one sister living, Thelma Louise Tune and two beautiful great nieces, Cara Louise and Cora Jean, who we call CJ. Thelma and I took turns taking care of the twins' mom while she was growing up. After she passed away, I raised CJ and Thelma raised Cara until they turned fourteen. They spent the rest of their adolescence and teen years together. Once they became adults, CJ settled here in Truway and Cara made her home where she grew up as a child at Las Bonitas Ranch outside of Whistle Stop, New Mexico. Even though they don't see each other more than a few times a year, they are still exceptionally close.

This wedding has to be one of the most memorable events I've ever experienced in my years on this earth. Nothing compares to the emotions I am going through at this moment. CJ is marrying Austin Chilacothe, John Mark's grandson. Before I could think about all of the events that occurred prior to this day, I heard Brother Mike talking.

"Do you take Cora Jean as your lawful wife?" Brother Mike asked.

"Yes, I do," replied Austin.

"Then, please repeat after me," instructed Brother Mike.

"I, Austin, take you, C.J., to be my lawfully wedded wife, my constant friend, my faithful partner and my love from this day forward. In the presence of God, our family and friends, I offer you my solemn vow to be your faithful husband in sickness and in health, in good times and in bad, and in joy as well as in sorrow. I promise to love you unconditionally, to support you in your goals, to honor and respect you, to laugh with you and cry with you, and to cherish you for as long as we both shall live."

Austin repeated the vows word-for-word with no hesitation.

"Now, C.J., do you take Austin as your lawful husband?" Brother Mike asked.

"Yes, I do."

"Please repeat after me," said Brother Mike.

Before he could say another word, CJ started reciting the same vows to Austin from memory; however, she changed the ending "…and to love you forever as God directs our lives together."

Brother Mike smiled and said, "I now pronounce you husband and wife. Austin, you may kiss your bride."

The wedding ceremony and events surrounding this monumental event is unique in more than one way. First of all, it's a blessing that Austin is even here today after what happened yesterday. He decided to add rain gutters to the house he built for CJ. When he was at the top of the ladder, a squirrel decided to run down the roof and leap to the ground. His flight was interrupted by Austin's broad chest and both panicked.

Austin tried to knock the squirrel away and as a result, the ladder leaned sideways and it and Austin plummeted into a freshly painted white rose trellis. Later he told us it seemed to happen in slow motion, except the part when the squirrel leaped on him.

When he didn't show up for the wedding rehearsal, we knew something had to be wrong. Austin is never late for anything. CJ tried calling the house, but got no answer. Austin was also not one to let the phone ring and ring if he was in earshot.

"I have to go find Austin. Something must have happened to him." CJ howled.

As the search party, which was now the same as the wedding party, departed the church, John Mark drove up to the front steps in the farm truck.

"John Mark. Have you seen Austin?" CJ demanded, forgetting her niceties in her panic.

"Yes, as a matter of fact, I have. He had a fight with a squirrel and is now at the clinic getting a cast for his broken ankle. I came to tell you that he sends his love and apologies for being late, but not even a broken ankle will keep him from getting married to you tomorrow, CJ," John Mark replied. "And that's an exact quote."

"Oh, for heaven's sake. A fight with a squirrel?" CJ asked, skepticism and amusement playing tug-of-war in her voice.

John Mark told her about the event as he knew it and showed a particular cheer in describing how Austin turned up at the clinic with white diamond shapes painted all over himself from the trellis. As John Mark was telling the story, he began to chuckle. He turned and saw me standing behind CJ, and faltered, ending his story with a smile I could tell was meant only for me.

It was one of the few times I had seen John Mark since he lost Geraldine a year ago. She never got to come home after her stroke in 1971. I can't believe that a heart attack took her life.

It was wonderful to see him again. Those clear blue eyes haven't changed since high school. It was nice to see him laughing.

"CJ, I'll go with you to pick up Austin at the clinic. He may be in too much pain to go through a wedding rehearsal tonight." I told her, breaking the tension that wound up between John Mark and me.

"Thanks, Aunt Lottie!" CJ stammered as she wiped the tears off her cheeks. I hadn't been paying much attention to whether they were from relief or the gales of laughter she herself threw out after hearing John Mark's story.

Austin not only made it to the rehearsal, despite the doctor telling him it was best if he took the night off, he was able to stand beside CJ on his crutches as they became husband and wife today.

Brother Mike said he liked the fact that he wasn't the only one with crutches on stage for a change which brought a well-timed laugh from those gathered to observe the union. He has been on crutches since being born with Cerebral Palsy.

After the ceremony ended, I looked around the room and saw the expressions on my loved ones faces. Thelma, was of course, crying. Cara was smiling at her sister, with just a hint of tears in her eyes. Glen was smiling, too, but instead of looking at CJ, he was gazing at Cara. There's something about the way Cara looks at the people she loves that reminds me of Betsy Grace. Their expressions are identical.

Betsy Grace was my oldest sister and I realize just how much I miss her.

I say "was" because I don't know if she is alive or dead. I haven't heard from her in a very long time. CJ and Cara don't know anything about her. I've often wondered what might have happened to her. She was Jean's mother and the twins' grandmother, but I haven't spoken her name out loud since she left. She'd been gone for 40 years to pursue her singing career in Nashville. She never looked back or contacted us as far as we know after she left. We tried to contact her, but every attempt we made was to no avail.

It's so difficult to forgive her for leaving, but I'll always love her, and I guess loving someone is part of forgiving. One day I will tell the girls about their beautiful, talented grandmother. Just like I will tell them about the relationship between the Trinity's and Chilacothe's.

Secondly, the Trinity and Chilacothe families have been in Truway for over three generations, but their interactions have been strained in the past. Now there is a union between the two families.

No one will be able to say that they were like the "Hatfields and McCoys" or the "Montagues and Capulets" any longer. No, siree, these two young people were going to rewrite history.

Someday I will tell CJ and Cara about the past connections between the families, but that's a story that'll have to wait. Look at me, "Auntie Secret".

* * *

"Aunt Lot-t-t-tie!" CJ called waving her bouquet in my direction. "What are you daydreaming about? I have tried to get your attention for the last five minutes." She hesitated, considering, "Well, maybe it hasn't been quite five minutes, but it sure seemed like it."

"I'm sorry, CJ," I said as I walked over to hug her and Austin's necks.

"I was just thanking God for this day. Who would ever think that one of the Trinity girls would marry a Chilacothe?" I laughed.

CJ gave me her remarkable smile, one that lights up her entire face, and reminded me of Jean whenever she was caught mid-mischief, then turned to see Cara and Glen standing next to Austin.

"Cara, you have no idea how happy I am at this moment," she exclaimed.

"Oh, I think, I can. It shows on your face. You're so radiant, probably the most gorgeous bride I have ever seen. Correction, you are the only bride I have ever seen, but still absolutely stunning."

Cara told her.

"Congratulations, you two." Glen said. "We look forward to you taking time to visit Las Bonitas Ranch before you come back to normal life."

"We're excited, too. I promised Cara that we would be at the ranch to help with the grand opening of Victory Bound Campground and by golly, we will. We're going to hang out with you for two weeks after a brief honeymoon in Las Vegas, New Mexico. Austin and I want to spend our honeymoon at the Plaza Hotel like Mama and Daddy did before we head out to the ranch," CJ explained.

"That's outstanding. Thanks for the help in getting the camp started. Cara and I have been anxiously waiting for this opportunity for over a year. It's hard to believe that we will finally open," Glen said.

"CJ," said Cara, "I'm so thrilled to be starting the camp with you by my side, however, I am infinitely more excited about today, yours and Austin's wedding day. June 5, 1982 is the big day now."

Finally, the "icing on the cake", happened when we had an unexpected guest arrive.

As we made our way into the reception hall, I heard a shrill voice yelling, "Austin, I'm so happy for you. You are dazzling in that tuxedo, I might add. What do you think about the dress I chose to wear to your wedding?"

"It's nice, Sally Jane. CJ and I are glad you put our special day on your busy calendar." Austin replied.

"CJ, who is Sally Jane?" I whispered in her ear. She whispered back, "She's Austin's cousin. Her last name is Nelson. We met in school, but we never really became friends, but there's a reason why."

Before CJ could explain we heard Ted Johnson hollering at the top of his lungs, "Clear the way. My prize pig got out of his pen and someone accidently let him into the reception hall and he's running wild!"

We stepped aside just in time to see his award-winning hog come barreling through the crowd. Several people fell down and we witnessed another person being knocked into the refreshment table.

Fortunately, Mr. Johnson was able to chase the pig out the side door while the rest of us surveyed the damage. At first glance, the mess didn't seem to terribly awful until we saw Sally Jane Nelson sitting on top of Austin's German Chocolate cake crying. The table it was supposed to be on was turned upside down and the cake ended up on the floor. Mr. Johnson's prize pig obviously ran into Sally Jane and caused her to fall back onto the cake. I guess we can at least say Austin's favorite dessert broke her fall. I don't think she saw any good in the situation because she was screeching at the top of her lungs, "I can't believe that I've ruined another dress from Paris while spending time with you, CJ Trinity."

"That's why we never became friends." CJ said trying not to smile.

Even though we had lots of commotion with Mr. Johnson's pig, CJ and Austin eventually cut the wedding cake and fed each other the traditional first bite. We laughed and danced the rest of the evening celebrating the union of two of Truway's finest people.

* * *

The newlyweds skedaddled as soon as the reception was over. I miss them already, but know they will eventually be back. They not only have the farm to look after, they have my three businesses to operate. Lou Ann Brown and her girls, Emma Lou and Bea will help me with the businesses and I reckon John Mark will have Jas Luke look after the day-to-day operations on the farm while they're out of town, but we need them to come back soon. They really run the show around here.

John Mark and Jas Luke live in their big white house on the Chilacothe Farms by themselves. Bernice, Austin's mother, left town right after she was released from a mental hospital in Del Rio. She just couldn't cope with the fact that she was partly to blame for Jean's death. Knowing that she spiked Jean's chocolate candy she gave her with a poison was too much for her to handle. Austin goes to see her every

Christmas. CJ finally went with him last year to let her know that she and Austin were going to be married. Bernice was invited to the wedding, but chose not to come. I just hope the demons she is living with will leave her in peace someday.

Austin moved out of the big farm house over a year ago so that he could build the house for him and CJ closer to town. He put so much of himself into their new house, even surviving his fall before the wedding. The house is located just a hop-skip-and-a-jump from my house so I'll be able to go by and water the flowers and plants around the house every day while Austin and CJ are in New Mexico.

I'll have to get up with the sun in order to get everything done, but that's okay. It's nice to be needed again at Big Southern Hair.

* * *

Can you believe it!? I accidently dyed three people's hair hot pink today. And of course, one of them would have to be Gertrude Jones. She told me that since she has left the Big Southern Hair & Highlights with hot pink, cotton candy hair, not once, but twice in her lifetime, she would have to find another beauty salon even if it meant driving all the way into Del Rio.

I'm disappointed in myself for not realizing that I put bleach into the applicator bottles just like CJ did when she was 13, but I have to say that it sure is going to be quiet for a change in the salon with Gertrude gone. She certainly likes to tell people about everyone's business whether we want to hear it or not. She doesn't know it, but Lou Ann took a picture of her reflection in the mirror with a look of horror on her face before I was able to apologize for the hair mishap--again.

Our 50th high school reunion will be next year and it would be so much fun to show our classmates Gertrude in her hot pink hair, but I don't think she would appreciate that, so I will take the high road and put the picture in an album at home. When I'm feeling low, I can always get it out and reminisce about the pink hair days and Gertrude's promise to ban Big Southern Hair for the rest of her life.

* * *

I got a letter from CJ. She said they were helping Cara and Glen get ready for the opening of the Victory Bound Campground. What a special time for them. Victory Bound will be for Marfan syndrome kids and adults, as well as their families.

Marfan syndrome, known as Marfans, is a genetic disorder that affects the connective tissue in the human body. Providing the camp is the way Cara and Glen, also two people with Marfans chose to support the research started by the Foundation in Port Washington, New York.

The camp mascot is Sam, the snow-white burro who is like family to all of us. I swear he's almost human. He seems to understand everything that's said. He's close to 30 years old now. It's hard to believe that he has been around as long as Cara and CJ have been alive. His adventures with the girls will continue for many more years to come. Burros are known to live for 50 years or more. I'm glad he will be around for the kids at camp, as well as, the girls' own children.

Tomorrow I'll have the opportunity to re-dye two of our customers' hair. I offered to fix Gertrude's hair, too, but she declined my services. Maybe I'll put that picture up in the salon after all.

Chapter 2
Victory Bound Campground
(Thelma, 1982)

**"We're on the road to Victory,
no matter how long it takes!"
Lyrics from Victory Bound**

I am content this morning as I sit here on my front porch drinking egg coffee and watching the sunrise casting shades of orange, pink, and yellow over the Las Bonitas Ranch. Who would ever believe that by putting a raw egg in coffee grounds would keep them from floating around in the cup. We learned the "egg" trick from our mama. She would make a piping hot cup of coffee for daddy every morning before he went to work for Mr. Chilacothe. She said her mama told her that the best way to keep the coffee grounds from floating to the top and ruining the coffee was to put the egg in the pot while the coffee was brewing and the egg kept the grounds on the bottom. Imagine that?

We plan to eat breakfast at the Whistle Stop Cafe. It's been awhile since I ate one of Joe's famous breakfast tacos. It will be interesting to see what Austin and Glen decide upon for their first meal of the day. Of course, Cara will join me in devouring the breakfast taco while CJ chows down on Jean's Delight. What a special memory for the girls to have these delicacies named for their parents.

Once we finished our food and enjoyed each other's company, Cara said, "We better be on our way back to the ranch and complete our finishing touches on the Victory Bound Campground.

If you're traveling west out of Whistle Stop, New Mexico, you're destined to see the new sign hanging from the gate that leads to Las Bonitas Ranch. It says, "*Welcome to Victory Bound Campground—Home of Sam, the snow-white burro!*"

The first day of camp is tomorrow and even though we've all been working hard to get everything ready for our campers and their families, it seems like we're still not quite through with what needs to be done. Ready-or-not, our first campers will arrive tomorrow just after daybreak.

Cara and Glen have burned the midnight oil preparing for the first day. CJ and her new husband, Austin have worked right along beside them getting things ready for our campers.

Even Sam has carried materials from one side of the camp to the other for days. I can tell that he is proud of his contributions. He's always been part of the family.

My name is Thelma Louise Tune. I am the owner of Las Bonitas Ranch and one of the directors of the Victory Bound Campground.

It has been such a blessing to plan not only the grand opening for this one-of-a-kind camp, but also designing the camp has been rewarding. We have been working tirelessly for a year and I am amazed at what we have been able to accomplish.

The campground is located only a quarter of a mile from our house. We contracted with a local company run by the brother of our ranch foreman, Juan, to customize the campground. The builders did a remarkable job. We have two large cabins, one for girls and one for boys. There's a bathroom and 50 bunk beds in each cabin.

Between the cabins, there's a huge recreation building which includes the dining hall and a special big room for arts, crafts, and games. We included a shelf with over 300 books for the campers to read on rainy days even though rainy days are rare in New Mexico.

At the back of the camp, there's a lake which will be a place for canoeing and kayaking. We want to add paddle boats later.

There's a barn which houses our horses and of course, Sam. Behind the barn is a tractor with a trailer that we plan to use for hay rides around the ranch. There's an archery range, a field for egg and three-legged races, and an outdoor stage for musical performances and plays.

Lest we forget, we need to thank God for his help in putting this campground together, too. Now, if only I could wind down enough to get some shut-eye before campers start showing up.

* * *

The big day arrived with the most spectacular sunrise we had seen in a while. We all lined up to greet our guests as they drove into the Victory Bound Campground. All the campers, their families, and friends seemed to pull up in front of the recreation building at the same time.

The first family to walk up was the Sanders family. Brothers Carson and Hudson were going to be staying with us for two weeks. Next up was the Tomes family with their two girls, Carrington and Collyns. Carrington and Collyns applied to be on our staff of counselors for the entire summer before heading off to Highlands University in Las Vegas. This was their second visit with us. They came at the end of May for their training. The others drove up right behind the Tomes.

Carrington and Collyns greeted their fellow colleagues with hugs and smiles. The counselors who would be staying with the boys were Jet, Jason, Justin, and Nathan.

The other two camp leaders for the girls, Chelsea and Tara would not be here until next month because we didn't have as many girls signed up for the first session. Cara plans to stay in the girls' cabin for a few nights just to make sure everything is going smoothly.

One by one, the rest of the campers arrived with their families in tow. After a welcome speech given by Cara and Glen, we all went out to a picnic area by the lake and had lemonade as people took turns introducing themselves.

The families bid farewell to their children and drove out the gate trusting us to take care of their most prized possessions.

"Well, here we are on our first day." Cara said. "What do we want to do first, get settled into our bunks and change into our camp tshirts before taking a tour of the camp?"

"That sounds like a great idea." Glen chimed in.

The counselors called out the names of the kids on their lists and proceeded to the cabins for an hour of setting up their bunk area, storing their gear, and changing into their camp attire. The tour lasted until dark since there were lots of questions about everything they would be doing.

Speaking of Sam, I have to say, he stole the show tonight. As we were sitting around a campfire singing camp songs, like *Row, Row, Row Your Boat*, Sam came trotting around the circle waving his head to the group. Everyone started laughing and that made Sam run around the circle more braying at the top of his lungs.

It had been a wonderful day, and by God's grace, and our hard work, tomorrow promises to be even better.

* * *

Camp had been in session for three days when someone special joined us at Victory Bound. Juan knocked on the front door to the house very early that morning, which was not unusual. Sometimes we like to sip coffee in the mornings as we talk about the goings-on on the farm.

"Hi, Juan." I said as I opened the door and gave him half of a smile that turned into more of a yawn. Even if this was a tradition, we usually started a little later in the morning.

"What brings you here so early this morning. I hope all is well with the animals. Sam's okay, isn't he? I continued through my yawn. Just as I was asking about Sam, I noticed two little feet standing behind him.

"Juan, there's a small someone standing behind you. Who might that be?"

He reached behind and took the arm of the little person and put him in front of himself.

"Miss Thelma, this is my niece's boy, Charlie Jay. His mom had to go to Mexico to help take care of my mother, and asked if I could take care of Charlie Jay."

"That's great, Juan. He looks a little like you except for that mass of curly hair. That must've come from someone else. I know you'll have fun with him on the ranch," I said.

"Yes, he's loved being on the ranch, but my mom has taken a turn for the worse, and I need to go to Mexico, too. I know this is a lot to ask, but would you mind so terribly much taking Charlie Jay for a few days until I get back?" Juan said.

I didn't hear Cara walk up behind me. As soon as she saw Charlie Jay, she knelt down and said, "Hello, there. Would you like to come in and have pancakes with us? And guess what, we are going to have breakfast tacos tomorrow with lots of other kids in our camp." She exclaimed with a smile.

Charlie Jay wrapped his arms around Cara's neck and then kissed her on the cheek. She picked him up and carried him into the house.

"Juan, I guess that answers your question. It looks like Charlie Jay and Cara are already the best of friends. You go see about your mom and know that we will take very good care of your little guy." I remarked.

"Thank you so much, Miss Thelma. I will try to get back as fast as I can. My brother can't leave due to his construction business. He said he would come out here every morning with some of his crew to take care of the horses and Sam while I am away."

"Don't worry about anything, Juan. We will pitch in to help. As a matter of fact, I think it would be a good idea to add taking care of the animals to the list of the things the campers will do."

"Muchas gracias, again, Miss Thelma. My madre's heart has been weak for a while. She needs her children close," Juan continued.

We both looked back at the house as we heard Cara and Charlie talking. They came back to the front porch to tell Juan goodbye. He tousled Charlie Jay's hair and turned to walk back to his truck. We are so happy to welcome this little guy to our family. It's going to be a special summer.

* * *

The first group of campers are scheduled to leave in a few days, but not before we all have a show on the stage. Each counselor and his or her kids have been working on their performances for over a week.

Two of our campers, Carson and his brother, Hudson have embraced all of the scheduled events. Glen showed me a copy of a letter that Carson wrote home about his camp experience:

Dear Mom and Dad,

I am having a great time at camp. We are doing a lot of fun activities. The obstacle course is my favorite. I am also meeting a lot of new people and making new friends. We are getting to kayak and fish. I caught one the first week I was here!

I do miss home, but just a little bit. See you soon, and I love you.

Sincerely, Carson

PS Hudson said to tell you, "hi".

It warms my heart to know the camp is being enjoyed by everyone. Little Charlie Jay has been a delight and has fit in well with us. He follows Cara around all day long and waits for her to read to him every night before he goes to bed. I see an expression on her face when she looks at Charlie that seems to be reserved just for him.

I was sitting on my porch swing basking in the beautiful sunshine then turned my head when I heard someone running up the front steps.

"Aunt Thelma, I want to do a performance on our last night with Austin, Charlie Jay and Sam. Do you want to join us? Glen says he will be our stage manager and emcee for the group." Cara said.

"Sure. It'll be fun. Do you have an idea about what we'll do?" I asked.

"Well, I've always liked the song, *He's Got the Whole World in His Hands.* Charlie Jay could help make a paper Mache world with blue and green paint. We can teach him to hold it up as we sing the chorus. Do you have any old party dresses that we could wear for the occasion?" Cara asked excitedly.

"There's an old trunk in the attic with dresses we once wore when we were performing.

We'll go up and look at what's available right now. I hope the moths haven't ruined them." I replied.

"What do you mean, when you were 'performing'?" Cara inquired.

"Oh, that's a long story and one that needs to be told when we are snowed in this winter while having an apple cider." I laughed, trying to brush off my slip-up.

We went up into the attic while CJ stayed on the porch swing with Charlie Jay. Cara opened the trunk and gasped at what was inside. "These are amazing dresses. Were they made by hand?"

"Yes, as a matter of fact they were. Our best friend, Ray Nell Benedict asked her mom to sew them for us. She had a job making clothes for many of the folks in Truway. Her talent was exceptional." I remarked.

"Aunt Thelma, there's something caught in the lining of the trunk. Do you see it?" Cara asked.

I peered into the gap between the trunk and lining that had apparently been ripped away. I pulled on it and could not believe what I held in my hand.

"Cara, this is an old record of us singing our theme song called *Southern Grit & Glamour.* That also happened to be the name of our group. I thought it was lost a long time ago. We had so much fun back then singing in church and for special events in and around Truway."

"Do you think it will still play?" Cara asked.

"There's only one way to find out. Let's go down and put it on the stereo and see what happens."

The record was a little scratchy, but we sang like we'd never sung before. Listening to this song brought back so many memories. My eyes teared up as I closed them to relish every note. As the tears began running down my cheeks, Cara walked over and put her arms around my neck.

"Aunt Thelma, who's singing this song with you. It's beautiful!" I opened my eyes and realized that I would have to tell her whose voice was unmistakably the most gorgeous one of all.

"Cara, this is me, Aunt Lottie, our friend, Ray Nell, and my oldest sister, Betsy Grace." Betsy Grace is the lead singer on the record and she was your grandmother.

"Wh-wh-at?!" Cara stammered. CJ came into the house at that moment with Charlie Jay. She saw the tears on my face and the look of astonishment on Cara's. "What's going on?" She asked.

"Our grandmother, Betsy Grace, was the lead singer in the sisters' band called, *Southern Grit & Glamour.*" Cara explained. She indicated the stereo which had fallen silent even though the record still spun, the needle had slipped off the vinyl.

I looked at CJ and then back at Cara. "We have a lot of catching up to do in regard to Betsy Grace, but now we have campers who need us. I'll tell you everything once the campers are gone in two days." I said and then walked briskly out the front door.

* * *

We performed our songs and skits for the families on the last camp day. Everyone got standing ovations. The families were more than happy to buy talent show tickets. All proceeds from the show went to The Marfans Foundation in the hope for new research that would make for better futures.

However, we were unable to have our hotdog and S'mores after the show. Someone raided the camp refrigerators in the kitchen and took all of the hotdogs, buns, marshmallows, graham crackers, and chocolate candy. We questioned all of the counselors that evening and they talked to their campers to see if we could get any leads as to who would do such a thing, but we never were able to solve the mystery. Who would have come into our camp and stolen food from us? The campers have given our unwanted guest a name. They call him the "S'more Thief." Let's just hope we've seen the last of food being removed from the premises without our permission.

* * *

The sunrise the next morning was amazing as only sunrises in New Mexico can be. We said goodbye to the campers. They were sad to leave, but excited about coming back next summer.

The girls and their fellas were exhausted from all that had taken place the last two weeks. Lucky for me, they went to bed early after the campers left and didn't ask me any more questions about Betsy Grace.

What do I tell them? I'll have to pray that God gives me the right words to say. Praying now before I hit the sack will be a good idea. I don't know the ending to the story, but I know it's going to be okay.

Chapter 3
Ollie Meets Ashley (Lottie, 1983-1993)

"Oh, Sweet Baby of mine!"
Lyrics from *Babies are the Most Precious Gift of All*

CJ and Austin returned home a few days ago from a rewarding trip to New Mexico for the Victory Bound Campground debut. I loved hearing the stories they had to share about the campers and their escapades.

I gave them some time to get back to their routine before returning to their house to officially welcome them back to Truway.

CJ was up early and off to check on our family's establishments this morning, but instead of going to the farm, Austin told her he had something special he needed to do in Del Rio. I spent last night with them so that I could fix a special welcome home dinner and a celebration breakfast this morning. John Mark came by yesterday to help me hang my "welcome home" banner across the front door before CJ and Austin came home from work. I invited him to stay for dinner, but he said he was on his way to Del Rio and wouldn't return until the next day. He asked me if he could take a rain check for another time, and I said, "Most definitely."

CJ walked into the kitchen later on in the morning after she told me she wouldn't be back until the afternoon.

"What's going on? I thought you weren't coming home until later today," I asked.

"I'm home for two reasons. I don't feel very well and decided I rushed into going back to work too soon after a tiring two weeks on the ranch. That's the first reason. The second is because Austin told me to meet him here for lunch. He said he had something to show me," CJ replied.

I reached out and hugged her to me for a few seconds and smelled the baby shampoo she has always liked. She pulled away slowly and smiled that remarkable smile of hers.

"Austin loves surprises. Let's just hope he hasn't decided to buy anything in Del Rio. We need to sit down and take a look at our finances and pay off this house before buying any new farm equipment," CJ continued.

While CJ went up to her room to lay down, I cleaned the kitchen and decided I would make a light lunch for her and Austin. I would quietly leave once I got the lunch ready so they could be alone to eat and share Austin's surprise. Before I could get everything ready, I heard Austin yell out, "Hey, where is everybody? CJ, Aunt Lottie, where are you?"

I walked into the living room, "Hi, Austin. CJ wasn't feeling too well, so she is taking a nap prior to lunch. I made you tuna fish sandwiches and tomato soup."

"Thanks so much, Aunt Lottie. You're so good to us. I don't know what we'd do without you. You're not going to believe what I brought home."

We heard CJ call out from upstairs, "Austin, is that you?"

Austin bound up the first few steps on the stairs even though he was still on crutches. "CJ, I need for you to come downstairs if you're feeling up to it. I want to show you something."

She came down the stairs very slowly, but she couldn't help smiling at her husband. "Austin, please tell me you didn't buy a new tractor," she sighed.

"A tractor! Why would I buy a new tractor now? Just because I was researching the John Deere brochures doesn't mean I want to buy one. I just like seeing what kind of gadgets the new ones have on them. That's all," he snorted.

Austin turned and walked out onto the front porch, bent down to pick up a box with holes in it and asked me I'd mind helping him to pick it up and give it to CJ.

"What's in the box?" CJ asked.

"Open it and find out."

I watched CJ's face as she opened the lid and peered inside. Her face went from a surprised look to one of gratitude mixed with disbelief.

"Austin, what have you done? Is this precious dog for me? We can't really afford to have a pet right now, you know. He's adorable, but I don't know. Puppies are a lot of work. We're still setting up our home. How are we going to be able to do that, work, and take care of a dog?" She retorted.

"But he's awfully cute. What's his name?" CJ rambled on.

"What would you like to call him?" He asked.

"I like the name Oliver, Ollie for short," CJ broke out into a smile.

"CJ, just say 'thank you' and hug my neck. You know you already love Ollie. I see it on your face," Austin grinned.

"Aunt Lottie, what do you think about us raising Ollie at this time in our lives?" CJ implored.

"You always wanted a dog growing up, CJ. I never let you have one and I regret that. Do what Austin said, say 'thank you' and hug his neck," I replied.

CJ put the box down and ran over to her new husband and grabbed him around the neck.

"Thank you. I already love Ollie. You are a sly one, Austin Chilacothe. You knew I would've said no to a dog if you asked me rather than bringing him home without asking," she laughed.

As CJ was thanking Austin, Ollie climbed out of the box, scampered over to the plant beside the couch, knocked it over, and then ran under the couch to hide.

"Why is there a puddle of water beside the couch?" I asked.

"Uh, oh. I think I know now why I said 'no' to a dog for all those years. Good luck, CJ and Austin. I think this is the time I need to make my way home. Enjoy your lunch and Ollie," I said as I ran out the door.

* * *

I stayed home for a few days to catch up on housecleaning and reading, but decided I wanted to see how Big Southern Hair was doing. When I walked inside the salon, I noticed that all of the beauty operators were staring at the back room door.

"What are all of you staring at?" I asked.

"CJ was talking to us about the upcoming Chilacothe Farms festival plans one minute and the next minute she's hightailing it to the back room." Ella Mae said.

I walked to the back room and couldn't see her anywhere. "CJ, where are you?" I asked.

"I'm in the bathroom, Aunt Lottie. I just lost the egg-white omelet I had for breakfast this morning," she replied.

"What's wrong with you, girl?" I asked her.

"I don't know. Maybe I should go see Dr. Thompson and get a checkup," she sighed.

* * *

The next morning, CJ and I went to breakfast at Jean & Joe's Place. She decided against one of her favorites, Joe's Burrito and opted for the cream of wheat and dry toast instead. I had Jean's Delight which is a soft taco with an egg, bacon, and cream cheese with green chilies. As we waited for our food to arrive, CJ smiled at me and said, "It's so nice to sit here across from you at one of my favorite places."

I brushed her cheek with my fingertips and asked if she wanted to say a prayer about her doctor's visit. She nodded with tears in her eyes. We joined hands and I asked our dear Lord to wrap his ever-loving arms around CJ.

After breakfast, I went to the salon and CJ went to see Dr. Thompson.

When I arrived, Ella Mae said with a grin on her face. "Lottie, we sure do miss the pink hair days."

"Well, I don't." I said, but I smiled at the memory of the looks on the faces of the customers with pink hair.

We all laughed out loud and continued laughing until we saw CJ come in. The look on her face stopped us cold.

"CJ, what's wrong. Why are you crying?" I said as I made my way to her as quickly as possible.

"Is Austin here yet?" She asked.

"No, he isn't. CJ, you have to tell me what's wrong," I begged.

Just then Austin walked into the salon. He saw her tears and turned pale. "What did Dr. Thompson say?"

CJ looked at Austin then turned and looked at all of us standing there gaping at her.

She didn't say anything for what seemed like an eternity and then she replied, "He said, 'congratulations.'"

"Congratulations for what?" Austin asked in a whisper.

I knew what the "congratulations" was for. I put my hands up to my mouth and said, "Oh, my goodness, CJ, this is wonderful news."

"I don't get it. What's the wonderful…" Before Austin could finish his sentence, it dawned on him what was being said.

"You've got to be kidding, right?" He couldn't believe what he was hearing.

"No, I'm not. You're going to be a father and I'm going to be a mom. What do you think about that?"

Austin didn't say anything for a moment. Then as his eyes welled up with tears, he said, "I've never loved you more than I do right now, CJ Trinity Chilacothe."

They grabbed each other and laughed and cried for the next five minutes while we all laughed and cried with them.

* * *

Ashley Trinity Chilacothe was born on March 16, 1983 in the Del Rio General Hospital. Her sweet smile warmed our hearts from day one.

She has been an amazing addition to the Trinity and Chilacothe families. As soon as she was born she peered right into my soul when I held her for the first time. I don't know who she looks like more, CJ or Austin. Actually I think I even see a little bit of her aunt Cara when she smiles.

Her mannerisms are so much like her mother, always busy and happy on most days. Ollie took to her right away. If Ashley was crying, Ollie would howl until someone picked her up. When she started walking, Ollie followed her everywhere and continues to follow her wherever she goes today.

I'll never forget the time I was watching her for a few hours. Ollie was whimpering at the back door, so I let him out. As I turned to walk back into the kitchen, I heard a crunching sound coming from the corner by the basement door. When I peered over the island in the center, I watched Ashley put a piece of Ollie's dog food in her mouth and crunch away. After that, I suggested to CJ and Austin that they might want to feed Ollie on the back porch rather than in the kitchen.

Her first sentence was, "Kiss my grits!" She loves to sing songs and perform plays that she has created. Of course, there is always a major part for Ollie. My favorite was a play that she made up about a dog who could talk. She would cover her mouth with a hat when it was Ollie' part. What was amazing was how Ollie would stand perfectly still and then move his head as if he were talking during the play. Journal memories are the best memories of all.

* * *

Today's March 16, 1993. Ashley Trinity Chilacothe was born exactly 10 years ago to the minute. We're having her first double digit birthday party with all of the family members, including Cara, Thelma, Glen, and Charlie Jay.

John Mark has been here since daybreak. He seems to show up about that time most mornings just to tell Ashley he hopes she has a great day before she heads for school or off on one of her adventures.

Ashley's adventures remind me of her mama's when she was this age. Not to be outdone by her mother Ashley gave us quite a scare last week. She was out riding her new bicycle that John Mark gave her.

CJ told her to ride over to my house, then go to town, and return home.

Don't you know that little stinker decided to see how fast she could go and decided to ride the opposite direction toward Mount Hope Cemetery. As she neared the front gate just past the creek, it started to rain. Quicker than you can say "giddy-up," it began to rain so hard, Ashley couldn't see in front of her face. She was trying to get up the hill to the front gate, but her bicycle began sliding backwards. The rain was literally pushing her and her bike back down the road toward the creek.

She knew she had to make a quick decision. Did she stay with her new bicycle and possibly float down the creek or did she abandon the bike and climb the hill by foot and find shelter? She opted for the latter and ran as fast as she could through the front gate into Mount Hope. Just ahead of the gate was a crypt that had been placed there for the Jones' granddaddy.

When she looked back toward her bicycle, she saw it floating across the road and into Mill's Creek.

She would have to stay put and hope her mom and dad would come looking for her.

* * *

I came in the door and ran to answer the phone. "Aunt Lottie, this is CJ. Is Ashley at your house by chance?" she asked.

"No, she isn't. Why do you think she would be over here?" I asked.

"Oh, my word! You mean to tell me she didn't come over to show you her new bicycle?" CJ chirped. "No, I'm sorry to say she hasn't made it over here yet. Surely, she's at someone else's house in this storm." I hoped.

"I guess she might be over at Emma Lou's house. She wanted to show her and Ali Jane the bicycle, too, but I told her to go to your house today, ride around town, and then come home. That was 30 minutes ago," CJ cried.

"Don't worry. We'll find her. You call Austin and tell him what has happened. I'll call over to Emma Lou's house to see if she is waiting out the rainstorm over there," I assured her.

Emma Lou had not seen Ashley. I drove over to the house to see if she made it home. Austin was driving up at the same time. He had a bicycle in the back of his truck, but I didn't see Ashley anywhere.

* * *

"Ashley! Where are you? Please answer me Ashley." Her dad called out.

"Daddy, I'm here on top of the Jones' crypt." A sweet hoarse, voice answered weakly.

All of a sudden, I saw her mama and daddy running toward her faster than I've ever seen them move.

"Oh, Ashley. You're safe. I was so worried that the flood carried you down Mill's Creek with your bike," her mama cried.

"Wait a minute. Why are you sitting in the Mount Hope Cemetery? You weren't even supposed to come this direction from our house," she exclaimed.

"CJ, I happen to remember a time when you were 10 years old and ended up in this very cemetery during a tornado and Sherriff Tate found you in Mr. Cole's freshly dug grave. Do you remember that little piece of history when you were supposed to be ironing for Mrs. Avery, but decided to take a spin on your bicycle?" I said as I smiled at her.

"Mama, you never told me that story before. I want to hear more about your bicycle adventure. Maybe then mine won't seem so scary." Ashley said very quickly before CJ could answer me.

Austin touched CJ's arm and nodded at her. He picked Ashley up and put her on the ground just as the rain stopped.

"Well, I just wish Ollie had been with you. He would have led us to you sooner, and maybe I wouldn't be so angry and beside myself with worry." CJ said as she grabbed Ashley and held her to her chest.

"I love you so much, little girl. Now let's go home and hope that there won't be any more adventures for a while." She took one of Ashley's hands as Austin took the other and they walked toward their truck.

***

The birthday party had been going well. The kids were outside playing hide-n-seek, while we were in the house cleaning up the kitchen. We were remarking about what a nice party it had been when we heard a blood-curdling scream coming from outside.

Before we could go out to investigate, Emma Lou's little girl, Ali Jane came bursting through the door.

"Ashley sat on a snake while hiding behind the hedge. The snake crawled off. But now Ollie is chasing it across the yard." Ali Jane hollered.

When we all finally made it outside, Ashley was calling Ollie's name and trying to get him to come back. Ollie was determined to show that snake a thing or two, but it was frantically trying to get away as he barked and pawed at it. The good news is the snake wasn't a poisonous one. It was a rat snake, but Ashley didn't care what kind it was. She declared she would never play hide-n-seek again as long as she lived.

No more adventures, please, Lord. I'm 76 years old and my heart can't take much more. We would experience another event in our lives years later that would surpass everything that has happened to any of us thus far.

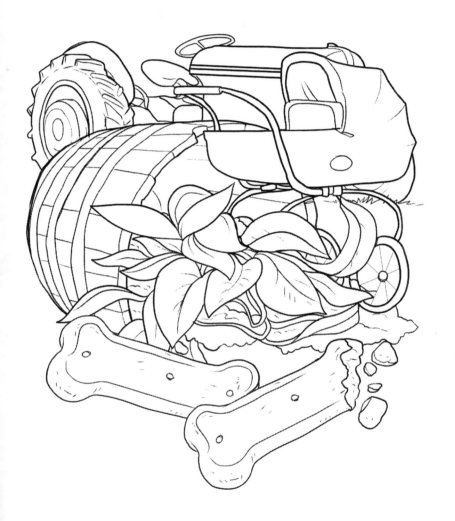

Chapter 4
Ollie, Sam, and the Gila Monster (Thelma, 1997)

"I will never forget your smile and the lingering laughter I still hear."
Lyrics from *The Best Friends are Sisters*

It's hard to believe that Victory Bound has been thriving for 15 years. We're starting our annual summer camps this week, and I'm especially thrilled that one of our original campers, Carson Sanders is now one of our camp counselors. Carson was diagnosed with Marfan syndrome when he was three and has a passion for helping others with Marfans. He has been coming to our camp every summer with his brother, Hudson since he was nine.

We contacted him last fall to see if he would be interested in being one of our counselors. He said, "Of course I'll be one of your camp leaders. Thanks for the opportunity to work with old and new friends at Victory Bound."

CJ has been sending Ashley with her dog, Ollie, to one of our camp sessions since she was ten. We told her we thought she was ready to help us out as a counselor, too, this year. Besides enjoying Ashley's company every summer, Sam took an instant liking to Ollie. The two of them are really funny to watch.

Last summer, Sam and Ollie took a tour of the ranch on their own. When they returned, they had red dirt all over themselves. They must've been caught in a dust storm because you couldn't tell what their original colors were for the amount of dirt on them. Ashley and Charlie Jay gave them baths, but there was still a hint of red for many days afterwards.

Charlie Jay has never left us since he arrived 15 years ago. His mom decided to stay in Mexico after her mother died. She has returned for visits, but doesn't stay long. She wanted to take Charlie Jay back with her after her first visit to the ranch, but when he showed her everything he was doing while living with us, she just couldn't take him away from Las Bonitas. It had to have taken a lot of courage to leave him with us rather than insisting he go with her. We will always be grateful to her for sharing him with us.

We love him like he was one of our own. He started his counseling role last summer.

One of the new attractions at Victory Bound is the archeological dig that the campers do as a part of their stay. Charlie Jay wants to map out a new area that we haven't surveyed before. He, Sam, and Ollie are out right now checking out the terrain further away from camp.

They've been gone longer than I anticipated. I hope nothing has happened to them. It seems that every few years, someone comes into our campground late at night and takes things on the last night the campers are here. After it happened the first time in 1982, we set up watch to see if we could catch the thief the next summer, but our mystery guest didn't take anything. He or she didn't show up again until 1987. That year all of the counselor's clothes and even the clothesline were taken. We questioned everyone in camp before they left the next morning, but no one saw anything unusual. Then in 1992, food was taken again. This year we're expecting our thief to return so we put all of the campfire cookout supplies in the refrigerator in the house. I hope Charlie Jay hasn't met up with someone who might rob him or heaven forbid hurt him.

When I went out to the front porch swing to look down the road, I saw Ollie running at break-neck speed toward the house. He stopped at the steps and let out the saddest, longest howl I've ever heard. Then he barked without stopping for several minutes.

"Ollie, what is it? Where is Charlie Jay and Sam?" I asked him like he could answer me.

He barked again and then turned and took off running away from the house. After a few yards, he stopped, turned his head and looked at me as if to say, "Well, aren't you coming?"

"Okay, Ollie, it's obvious you want me to follow you. Let's go to the barn and saddle up Betsy, Too and you can take me to find Charlie Jay and Sam." I said.

He took off to the barn. I swear that dog understands everything we say to him just like Sam does.

* * *

Ollie ran beside me and then stopped at the edge of Lost Man's Cliff. Sam was standing near the edge. As soon as he saw me, he brayed and then looked at something in the gulch.

"Charlie Jay, where are you?" I hollered. There was no response.

Both of the animals peered down over the ledge.

57

"Oh, no, guys, please tell me Charlie Jay didn't fall!" I cried.

"Charlie Jay, if you can hear me, please answer." I said as I began to cry.

"Aunt Thelma, I'm here. Step closer to the edge and maybe you'll be able to see me. I think my leg is broken so I can't stand up." I heard him say in a raspy voice.

"I'll ride back to the ranch and get help. Please hang on a little while longer. I'll get back as soon as I can. Sam will stay with you just so you know there is someone up here who loves you and won't leave you." I hollered through cupped hands around my mouth.

"Sam, you stay here with Charlie Jay. I'm going for help." Sam looked at me with an expression as if to say, "I will be on guard until you return."

Betsy, Too galloped as fast as she could go back to Las Bonitas. I found Juan and the family having lunch on the campground picnic tables.

"Charlie Jay has fallen off of Lost Man's Cliff. He thinks he has broken his leg. We need to get him up out of No Man's Gulch and to the doctor." I told them.

Juan gave everyone assignments after what seemed like forever and we were on our way to save our Charlie.

* * *

58

Poor Charlie, not only did he break his leg, but he endured one of the scariest moments of his life.

The following is an account of his story.

After I hit the bottom of the 10-foot drop off in No Man's Gulch, I knew there was something wrong with my left leg. It was hurting so much. I couldn't stand up on it. I looked up and I saw Sam's and Ollie's faces peering down at me.

"Ollie, go get help. I hurt my leg. Go home and get help." I heard one bark and I didn't see Ollie again. However, Sam stayed. I knew he would wait with me until someone came to help.

Suddenly I heard a sound. There was a good size boulder about 6 feet away from me. I heard a grunting, hissing sound coming from the other side of the huge rock.

Then I saw it. At first I thought it was a snake, but as I looked closer I could tell it wasn't a snake. It had yellow and black markings on its back and his thick forked tongue was flicking in and out. I knew immediately what it was. It was a Gila monster.

If I stayed still, maybe he would go away. They have a reputation of being very slow-moving, but are one of two poisonous lizards in North America. I looked at the top of the cliff. Sam was staring down, but now he seemed to be looking at the Gila monster rather than at me.

All of a sudden I was pelted by small rocks coming from the top. Sam was creating a small landslide of rocks and gravel. He was trying to scare the Gila monster away and it worked.

The lizard slowly turned and made his way back over to the other side of the boulder.

I scooted back as far as I could toward the 10-foot wall hoping to somehow hide in case the lizard decided to return.

I looked up and saw Sam nodding his head at me. "Way to go, Sam! I sure didn't want that lizard chewing on my hurt leg."

A few minutes later I heard Ollie barking in the distance. I was rescued.

* * *

Charlie's leg was broken not just in one, but two places. He didn't want us to postpone the first camp session, so everyone else is with the new recruits for Victory Bound while I am taking care of Charlie Jay.

"Would you like to have some lemonade?" I asked.

"That would be great. Thanks, Aunt Thelma. Would you also be up for a game of checkers?"

"Checkers sound like a good idea." Ashley said she would take over his campground duties, as well as her own, until he got his cast off.

"Aunt Thelma, I told Ashley that I saw something peculiar when I was lying in No Man's Gulch. I saw what looked like an entrance to a cave, probably the same one where the Gila monster lives. It was mostly covered with rocks except at the very top and the right-hand bottom corner. There was something in the cave that was catching the sunlight and shining in my face. Maybe someone dropped something off the cliff and an animal carried it to the entrance. I sure wish we could get back down there to investigate further," he continued.

"Maybe Juan could talk to some of the ranch hands to see if there's another way to get to No Man's Gulch. I don't know of another way to get down there."

Juan said that there was a trail leading to the gulch from the other side and he'd be glad to go find what Charlie Jay might have seen.

Later that evening when Juan returned he showed us what he thought Charlie saw in the corner. It looked like a charm from a bracelet or a pendant from a necklace. "Have you ever seen this before?" He asked.

I gasped as I looked at the pendant in his hand. "Let me get a better look at it, Juan." I said.

What I held in my hand couldn't possibly be what I thought it was. My sister, Betsy Grace had a pendant just like this one that she wore around her neck. It was given to her by her husband the day before his plane crashed in Truway. Could it be the same pendant?

"Aunt Thelma, what do you have in your hand?" Ashley had walked into the house and overheard us.

"It's a piece of jewelry I think belonged to your great grandmother." I said as I walked over to the couch to sit down.

"May I see it?" She asked.

I handed it to her and watched her face as she studied the pendant.

"Where did you find it?" She implored.

"I saw it when I was waiting for my rescue at the opening of what seemed to be a cave entrance I was telling you about." Charlie Jay said excitedly.

"I want to go see this cave entrance. Juan, can you take some of the campers and me to the back entrance to the gulch? After all, Charlie wanted us to dig in the area for artifacts. We might find pottery shards and maybe even another piece of jewelry."

She reminds me so much of her mother, but she looks a lot like her aunt Cara. She was on a mission and couldn't be persuaded to wait.

* * *

The next day Ashley and her team of "archeologists" took off for the long hike to the back of No Man's Gulch. I can't wait to see what else they find.

It was almost dark when Ashley made her way back. I was on the front porch swing staring down the driveway wishing for her to return.

As she got closer, she gave me one of her sideway grins which quickly changed to a serious look. "Hello, sweet Aunt Thelma.

You won't believe what we found in the cave. Charlie Jay was right. There was a cave entrance.

It took a couple of hours for us to remove the rocks from the entrance, but we persevered watching for that ole' Gila monster as we worked.

Right inside the cave we found a torn-up boot just lying on the cave floor. There was a dirt and gravel pile past the boot so we shoveled the pile to the other side to see what we might find."

Ashley paused to take a breath. Her eyes filled with tears as she held out her hand to me. Inside her hand was a ring, a ruby ring with diamonds surrounding the beautiful red stone. The inscription on the gold band said, "To BGT, From TFB."

"Where was this ring?" I asked in a shaky voice.

"It was attached to a skeleton of a hand under the dirt and gravel pile inside the cave!"

Ashley said excitedly.

I don't know how I remained standing, but somehow I found the inner strength to control my emotions.

I opened my mouth to tell Ashley more about the ring, but instead said, "Come into the house and get something to drink. I'm sure you're exhausted after your day of discoveries." I walked beside her and put my arm around her and hugged her close to me.

When we were almost to the front door, we heard a loud crash and I almost jumped out of my shoes.

"What on earth was that?"

"Aunt Thelma, come quick!" We heard Charlie say from the pottery studio. Ashley obviously got her second wind. She sprinted toward the studio like she was running the 100 meter dash.

By the time I got there, I noticed several broken pottery pieces lying on the floor. Ashley and Charlie Jay were reading something, but looked up with big eyes when I walked in. "What happened in here?" I asked.

"I'm so sorry. When I came through here from the backyard to see if Ashley had returned, my crutch hit the bottom of the shelf and everything came tumbling down," said Charlie Jay.

This note was in one of your vases that's now broken on the floor." His hand shook as he handed it to me.

January 15, 1943

Thelma,

I can hardly wait to see the look on your face when you read this note.

You were right. There's no way I can leave Jean even for a few weeks to pursue a singing career. I plan to meet Tom Frank tonight and tell him I'm not going to Nashville with him. He's not going to be happy, but I can't help it. I love my family too much to leave them. I'm giving him the ring back. I saved your life one day many years ago and now you've saved mine. Thank you! Wish me luck, Sis!

Love and appreciate you,

Betsy Grace

I couldn't believe what I was reading. Betsy Grace never left the ranch all those years ago. She was buried in a cave in No Man's Gulch. I thought she abandoned us and she didn't. What happened to her? How did she die?

Oh my, oh my, what's Lottie going to say when I tell her?

Chapter 5
Back in Thyme
(Lottie, 1929-1938)

*"We've no less days to sing God's praise
than when we'd first begun."*
Lyrics from *Amazing Grace*

The last time I sat in my Sunday pew with my entire family was when Austin and CJ married sixteen years ago in 1982. This time we're not celebrating the union between two people, but saying a final goodbye to our sister, grandmother, and great grandmother, Betsy Grace. As I sat there and listened to Brother Mike, my mind started drifting to a different time, a time when we were all girls growing up together.

I remember a hot steamy day when we decided to go swimming in the lake near our house, Lake Walk, after church. I always liked the name of the lake since it was a short *walk* from our house to the lake.

The year was 1929 just before the Great Depression began in October. We lost our daddy right after the end of World War I in 1918 which was also the year of the Great Flu Epidemic. Daddy had only been home for three days when he died, not from a wound fighting in the war, but from the flu.

Thelma was born that year, too, but not until Daddy died, so she never got to know him. I barely remember him since I was only two when he left us. The only thing Betsy Grace remembered was how he loved to let us ride around the house on his back while Mama was cooking in the kitchen.

Betsy Grace was born in 1915 so she was three when we had Daddy's funeral. After his passing, we moved out of the farmhouse near Chilacothe Farms. Before the war Daddy worked on the farm and was in the fields when Mr. Chilacothe rode up on his horse and announced that they would be growing a new herb called "thyme." He believed it would boost his sales so there was a lot of excitement about all the possibilities of using thyme in the vegetables grown on the farm.

The addition of thyme to the vegetables made Chilacothe Farms a place on the map. Mr. Chilacothe was so excited he decided to begin an annual celebration, the Chilacothe Farms Festival. Daddy never got to see the first festival called "The Best Thyme of our Lives".

Mr. Chilacothe liked the theme so much, he stuck with it every summer for 50 years. The festival was quite an event and we had special memories of it every year. More about the festival later...

On this particular day in 1929, Mama was resting as she always did after our Sunday lunch of ham, cornbread, and pinto beans and just a smidge of chowchow. I remember Betsy Grace calling out to me from outside.

"Lottie, go get Thelma and tell her to come out to the porch." I never questioned Betsy. She was the oldest and therefore, the wisest in my eyes. She was fourteen, I was thirteen, and Thelma had just turned eleven. Thelma must have heard her name mentioned because I didn't have time to fetch her before she appeared on the back screened porch where we slept in the summertime.

"What's going on?" She asked.

"How would you like to go down to Lake Walk and cool off with a swim?" Betsy Grace asked us both.

"Mama told us we can't swim without an adult around." I reminded her.

"I'm almost an adult so I say it's okay to go. Besides Mama had a long week. We don't need to wake her up and ask if we can go swimming." Betsy said.

Mama worked two jobs in town. During the week, she worked at the Truway Beauty Shop and on the weekends she worked in Della's Diner with her best friend, Tallulah Belle. Della only opened for breakfast on Sunday mornings so that everyone had a chance to go to church at the nondenominational church down the road. Mama's dream was to someday own the beauty shop. Della told her she couldn't continue to run both businesses and she liked Mama's work ethic, so she offered to sell the shop to her for a modest sum.

We did the laundry and cooking most days at home, not only for ourselves but for the next door neighbors, the Avery's. They paid us to help them out so we tried to save all of Mama's earnings for buying the beauty shop in the future.

As I said, I didn't question my older sister; therefore, we all changed into our shorts and tshirts and took off running to the lake.

Betsy Grace was right, as usual, the water was so calm and cool today. I was swimming on my back and staring up at the clouds in the sky, counting my blessings when I heard Thelma cry out, "Help!"

Before I could figure out Thelma was going under, I saw Betsy Grace swim toward her like an Olympic swimmer. She grabbed Thelma by the head of the hair and pulled her up to the surface. "Don't fight me, Thelma. Lie still and let me take you to shore."

I swam to shore, too, so that I could see how I could assist in her rescue. When they got to me, I reached down to pull Thelma out of the water. "What were you doing in the middle of the lake?" I asked.

"I wanted to see if I could swim from one side to the other like Betsy Grace was doing. When I got to the middle, my left leg cramped and I couldn't swim anymore." She said as I wiped tears off her cheeks.

"Betsy Grace, you saved Thelma's life!" I exclaimed.

"Well, maybe someday Thelma will save my life. We're not going to mention this to Mama. She already has enough to worry about."

We went home, took off our wet clothes, and lay down on our beds on the back porch. The near-drowning episode was never discussed again until four years later when we were introduced to Della's niece from El Paso, Ray Nell Benedict.

* * *

I remember the first day we met Ray Nell. We liked her right away. She told us about a time when she was charged by a bull near her home. She had taken a short cut through a pasture on a particularly hot afternoon.

She'd been in town having an ice cream soda in the local drug store with a boy from her class. Time got away from her so she had to take the short cut.

She had no idea that the farmer who owned the pasture had a bull, and she also didn't know that red was a color that caused bulls to charge which just happened to be the color dress she wore.

"I froze in place when I saw that bull stamp his hooves and snort. I was almost to the fence, but I knew if I ran, he'd outrun me quicker that I could whistle so I stayed still. He charged and just stopped an arms-length away as I climbed under the fence. That's the scary part. The funny thing is going across the pasture was a shorter way home so I got there in time and didn't get in trouble with Mama." Ray Nell was laughing so hard she was crying as she bent down and put her hands over her knees.

"I've never told anyone that story until now." Ray Nell said. "I guess that means we'll be the best of friends since you know something about me that no one else does. You'll have to tell me a secret so we can be even" she continued.

It only seemed right that we tell her about Betsy Grace saving Thelma from drowning in 1929.

"You know what this means?" She asked.

"No, what does it mean?" Asked Betsy Grace.

"It means that we all have grit. Do you know what 'grit' is?"

"Are you talking about grits that you eat?" Thelma asked.

"No, I'm talking about a different kind of grit. I spend a lot of my time in the El Paso Public Library working part time and reading when I get a chance. 'Grit' is defined as 'firmness of character; indomitable spirit.'" Ray Nell said with confidence in her voice.

"In whose spirit?" Thelma asked.

"Not whose spirit, but 'indomitable spirit.' You know, 'strong, tough spirit,'" Ray Nell chuckled.

"Well, I know a great word, too," said Betsy Grace not to be out done by our new friend.

"I like the word, 'Glamour' which means 'the attractive or exciting quality that makes certain people or things seem appealing or special.' I saw it defined in one of those beauty magazines in the shop the other day." Betsy Grace said dreamily.

"They both sound like us." I chimed in. "I say there's a lot of grit *and* glamour in our character."

"That's it! I've been trying to come up with a name for our singing group. The 'Trinity Girls' just didn't do it for me. Ray Nell, how would you like to be a back-up singer in our group called, 'Southern Grit & Glamour?'"

"I like it. Count me in. When do we get to perform?"

Wouldn't you know the "The Best Thyme of our Lives Chilacothe Farms Festival" was only three weeks away. It was just enough time for us to teach Ray Nell our song we'd been singing at church, "Mercy and Grace." Maybe one day we'd make up another song to match our name, "Southern Grit & Glamour."

* * *

Not only did we win first place that year in the singing contest, we traveled to other nearby festivals and churches singing our hearts out. We harmonized quite nicely. Ray Nell played the piano. I taught myself how to play Daddy's guitar and we were approached by John Mark Chilacothe about being our saxophone player. Of course, Betsy Grace was the lead singer. Thelma stood in the back and made up motions to go with the songs as a back-up singer.

However, our band wasn't complete until the year Tommy Earl Nelson visited the next summer in 1934. He knew how to play drums and it only made sense for him to join us for the singing contest in the festival that year. Everyone from miles around would come out and pay to hear us perform.

Yesiree, that John Mark and Tommy Earl were great additions to Southern Grit & Glamour!

* * *

We were having such a good time that summer. We'd just finished performing at a watermelon festival in Del Rio when John Mark said, "Lottie, I sure do like playing the saxophone for you ladies."

"Thanks. We like you playing for us, too."

"Lottie, I hope you don't think I'm being too forward, but I sure would like to ask your mama if it would be alright for me to call on you next week. Would that be okay with you?"

I blushed three shades of red before I replied, "I'd like that very much, John Mark."

He called on me the next week and continued to come over to the house every week the rest of the summer. One night in late August, he knocked on the door and said, "Lottie, I have something to tell you. My parents are sending me to Austin to the University of Texas to major in agribusiness. My dad thinks it'll be a good idea for me to get a college degree before taking over the farm someday."

"Well, hopefully, you'll be coming home for holidays and I'll get to see you when you're home."

"Most definitely. When I'm home, you'll be at the top of my list of people to visit," he said.

I went to the bus station to tell John Mark 'bye. He didn't come home at all his first year. His friends said that his parents thought it best for him to stay in Austin with some of their friends for holidays and they'd go there to visit him in school rather than him driving back to the farm.

It just so happened that their friends had a daughter who was also at the University of Texas. Her name is Geraldine Nelson. The next thing I heard was that John Mark and this Geraldine Nelson were getting married. It had all been pre-arranged by the Chilacothe and Nelson families. I guess it just wasn't meant for John Mark and me to be together.

The ironic part is that Betsy Grace married Tommy Earl Nelson, a distant relative of the Nelson family in Austin. They had a little girl named after Thelma and me, Jean Louise in 1935. We love being Jean Louise's aunts!

Even though I missed John Mark and was depressed about the news of his forthcoming marriage, I spent as much time as I could with Jean. She was the most extraordinary little girl I'd ever known.

I didn't get to see John Mark until he was through with school. He returned home to help run the farm. Mama asked me to take a welcome home present over to their big white house.

"Mama, please don't ask me to take this gift to the Chilacothe's. Can't Thelma take it?"

"Lottie, Thelma can go with you, but you need to go over there, too. He's been a good friend and we need to honor him and his new wife," Mama replied.

So, on June 15, 1938, Thelma and I were walking to the Chilacothe farm when we witnessed one of the most devastating catastrophes ever.

We watched an airplane come spiraling down from the sky right in front of our eyes and crash in one of the Chilacothe fields between our house and the big white house. Once we got to the house, everyone was running out and screaming that it was Tommy Earl's plane that crashed.

I couldn't believe it! He had been getting in flying time so that he could be a pilot for the Chilacothe's. Poor Betsy Grace. She loved her Tommy Earl so much. Jean had lost her daddy at the age of three.

What a terrible day! God, please comfort our sister and her daughter. How can we let them know that we'll always be here? How can we convince Betsy Grace to get out of bed each morning without the love her life? Give us the strength to be by her side, Lord.

Chapter 6
Thelma's Memories of Betsy Grace (1925-1938)

"He sacrificed it all, so we wouldn't have to fall."
Lyrics from Mercy and Grace

Lottie seemed to be taking the news well. She didn't say anything when we drove into Truway and gave her the news about Betsy Grace's death. She just stared at me as I was telling her the story of how we found the pendant in the cave and Betsy's ring on the skeleton's hand.

I guess I was crying pretty hard as I was telling the story because just like she did when I was eleven and nearly drowned in Lake Walk, she wiped the tears off my cheeks and then sighed, "Thelma, we will find out what happened to our beloved sister."

As we said our final goodbyes at Mount Hope Cemetery, I remembered something Betsy Grace said to me that day at Lake Walk. "Maybe someday you'll save my life." She wrote in her last note that I had saved her life. Obviously, I didn't since she ended up in a cave in No Man's Gulch.

The last person to see her alive was the person who was responsible for her death, but could that have been Tom Frank Buchanan? He didn't know the territory and couldn't have figured out how to bury Betsy Grace in the cave. Also, the red ruby ring was still on her finger when she died, so she didn't have time to give it back to him before she died. Who would've wanted to hurt her? Was it an accident or did someone kill her on purpose for some insane reason?

* * *

My favorite memory of Betsy Grace was in 1925. We were sleeping on the back porch because of the summer heat. We'd been telling scary stories before dozing off to sleep. I must've woken up screaming because I heard Betsy Grace calling my name, "Thelma, it's okay. You had a nightmare. I'm sorry we told those scary stories. You're too young to hear those kind of stories right before bedtime. How about me singing you a song and sit with you for a while until you get sleepy?" She smiled at me in the moonlight.

I nodded at her and she sang a song called, "Mercy and Grace." It was a song she wrote herself and she was only ten at the time. She said that she hoped to teach it to us and ask our pastor if we could sing it at church one Sunday.

Her voice was the most beautiful I'd ever heard. I knew that night Betsy Grace's gift was singing to folks, making them happy inside as she sang.

* * *

We got the opportunity to sing in our church on many occasions and eventually were asked to sing in other churches in Buford County. Betsy Grace was our main vocalist, but she was always looking for ways to put us in the spotlight, too. I'll never forget the Sunday she planned for me to sing a duet with her.

We sang one of the songs she wrote, "My Love is True." Lottie accompanied us on her guitar as Betsy Grace and I harmonized. The entire church stood up and clapped for us when we finished. She took my hand and had me stand in front of her so that I could be acknowledged. As I stood there soaking in the praise, I thought about how lucky I was to have not one, but two sisters I admired. We always stood by each other through thick and thin.

Even when Betsy Grace and Tommy Earl were sweet on each other, she'd ask Lottie and me to go with them on their dates. We ate ice cream at Della's Diner, watched movies once a month in the theater downtown, and laid out on quilts in the backyard seeing how many star constellations we could name.

"Thelma, is that the Big or the Little Dipper right above us?" Betsy Grace asked.

"I think it's the Little Dipper because it seems small compared to the Big Dipper you showed me the last time we laid on the ground looking at stars," I replied.

"I don't think it's either one," said Lottie.

"What makes you say that?" I asked.

"I see a shape that reminds me of my guitar," Lottie grinned.

"You're just saying that to tease," I said as I sat up.

Before I could stand up to go into the house, Betsy Grace pulled me back down on the quilt and started tickling me. I laughed so hard I couldn't get my breath. As I struggled to breathe, she would stop for a moment and then start tickling Lottie, but would persevere in tickling both of us until one of us yelled, "Calf Rope."

That was an old saying we would say when we gave up and couldn't handle something any more. The memories of our childhood and teenage years were the happiest ones.

* * *

Our singing career took off when we were asked to perform in the Chilacothe Summer Festival in 1933. That also happened to be the year I think I saw Bonnie and Clyde in Truway. I was in Della's Diner one day picking up some food to take to everyone in our group rehearsing for the festival performance.

As I scanned the diner while waiting for Tallulah, the waitress to bring our order to the check-out counter, I saw a couple sitting in the back corner booth. They seemed familiar for some reason, but I couldn't remember where I'd seen them before. The woman was petite with blond hair and a stylish hat. The man was not much taller and was listening intently to something the woman was telling him. I got so caught up in watching them, I didn't hear Tallulah Belle call my name.

"Thelma, here's your order. What are you staring at?" She glanced at the couple and then she bent down and whispered in my ear. "Those two people

are from out of town and I swear they look like that couple who have robbed banks around Texas. I don't remember their names, but I know that's them."
Tallulah Belle said.

Later that evening when Mama came home from the beauty shop, she said, "I styled a lady's hair today from out of town. She said they were just traveling through, but she sure would like to get her hair fixed before moving on. She asked if she could prop her leg up while sitting under the hair dryer. Apparently she was in an automobile accident where a car battery exploded and the battery acid burned her leg.

The injury was so severe she walked with a limp."

"What was her name, Mama? Did she tell you her name?" I asked excitedly.

"Yes, she told me her name was Bonnie. She gave the biggest tip I've ever had since working at the salon."

Later that same night we heard on the radio that a bank in Oklahoma was held up by a man and a woman earlier in the week. The man was described as being small in stature and the woman with him had short, blond hair.

I don't know if it really was Bonnie and Clyde who visited Truway, but Tallulah Belle and I will always believe it was.

* * *

As my sisters and I grew older we spent less time with each other. Our singing performances dwindled as did our quality time together. Men became my sisters' central focus. Betsy Grace met and married Tommy Earl Nelson. Lottie was smitten with John Mark Chilacothe, and I wouldn't meet the man of my dreams until 1941.

Before that happened, both of my sisters experienced heartbreaking events. Tommy Earl was killed in a plane crash when his daughter was only three years old. John Mark left home to pursue a college degree in Austin and ended up marrying someone else his family picked out for him. Not only did he come home with his new wife the same year Tommy Earl died, they also brought home a son, Jas Luke who was already three years old. Apparently, John Mark married Geraldine Nelson right after starting college and little Jas Luke was born shortly thereafter.

After Tommy Earl died, Betsy Grace moved back home with us so that we could help with little Jean. Mama, Lottie, and I took turns helping out with Jean. Betsy Grace would start her day with a smile, but by lunch time her energy level seemed to drop most days. She would take a nap after eating and would perk up for an hour or two, but then she would go out to the front porch and swing with Jean for hours without saying anything to any of us.

* * *

We supported each other the best we could. Mama continued to work two jobs, but was able to buy the Truway Beauty Shop and changed the name to Big Southern Hair. It was so much fun to brainstorm names. Lottie is the one who actually thought about calling the salon Big Southern Hair. Mama liked the name as soon as she heard it, so Mama's dream of owning her own salon finally came true.

Early in the summer of 1941, Henry Tune came into town. He came to visit his grandparents on his mother's side when our eyes met at the Chilacothe Summer Festival. He sat in the front row when we gave one of our rare performances for the year. He was smiling at me from ear to ear. I noticed his ears because they really stuck out, but his gorgeous smile lit up his entire face. It was love at first sight.

When our performance was over, he walked up on the stage, stuck out his right hand, and said, "Hi, my name is Henry Tune."

"Is Tune your middle name or your last name," I asked.

"It's my last name. Why would you think it was my middle name?"

"Most of the guys in Truway go by their first and middle names. I just figured you did, too."

"Well, I don't. I like to give my first and last names out to people I meet, especially pretty girls," he grinned at me.

"Do you meet lots of pretty girls wherever you go?" I asked.

"I thought I did until tonight. You are by far the prettiest girl I have ever seen," he exclaimed.

My face turned as bright as the inside of a pomegranate as I stammered, "W-w-would you like to join us for hot dogs and lemonade?"

"I can't go anywhere with you until you tell me your name."

"It's Thelma, Thelma Trinity. And just in case you're wondering, Trinity is my last name, not my middle name."

"Glad to meet you, Thelma Trinity."

* * *

We saw each other every day that summer until the day he told me he had to go home to Whistle Stop, New Mexico.

"Thelma, I know we only met this summer, but I can't leave here without you. How would you like to visit my ranch in New Mexico?"

"I'd love to visit your ranch, but I can't go without a chaperone at my age," I said.

"You could go without a chaperone if you married me first."

"Henry Tune, are you asking me to marry you?" I asked.

"Yes, Thelma. I know you're the one I want to spend the rest of my life with, so what do you say?"

I hesitated for just a few seconds before grabbing him around the neck and whispering in his ear, "Of course, Henry. I would love to spend the rest of our lives on your ranch."

Betsy Grace came alive helping me plan for the wedding. She and Mama made my dress. Lottie was in charge of all the wedding details. She reserved the church for our wedding date and took care of the flowers and cake.

Henry and I said our vows on October 4, 1941 and moved to Las Bonitas Ranch outside of Whistle Stop,

New Mexico. We had so much fun taking care of the ranch, riding horses, and digging for pottery shards.

I was happy even though I got the scare of my life right after we moved to the ranch. Henry introduced me to two of his favorite animals, Samantha, a snow-white burro and Kitty, his horse. He gave them both to me as wedding presents. We set out on a beautiful fall day to see the ranch on horseback. Kitty and I were getting along very well and then the excitement began. A rabbit darted out from behind a cactus plant and startled us both. Before I knew it, Kitty reared up and if that wasn't scary enough, she turned around and headed back toward the barn. She ran faster than any race horse could ever run in a derby. I don't know how I managed to hang on, but I did. Henry rode up beside us, leaned over to grab Kitty's reins and just before we got to the barn door, he was able to pull on her reins and stop her from entering the barn at break-neck speed.

"Thelma, are you alright?" he asked breathlessly.

I tried to answer, but all I could do was stammer, "I-I-I'm okay, but I don't think I want to ride Kitty for a few days." He sighed and then started laughing. I never realized how refreshing his laughter was. What began as a near tragedy became a hilarious event as we both laughed so hard we were crying.

We had many great adventures together. After the runaway horse incident, we painted the barn. It took us three days to complete the job, but the journey was worth it. We loved eating our lunch in the hayloft and just before dusk, Henry would put up our brushes and rollers and then grab me and dance around while singing a tune in my ear. I told him he had the perfect last name since he loved to sing *tunes* all the time. On the day we finished the barn, we climbed the steps to the loft, ran out the door and jumped into a pile of hay to celebrate our "new" barn.

* * *

I'd never been happier in my life, but then we heard our president, Franklin Delaware Roosevelt, say on the radio, "Today, December 7, 1941 will go down in history as a day of infamy." Japan bombed Pearl Harbor.

Henry didn't wait for our country to come ask him to fight in World War II, he enlisted and was scheduled to be shipped to Africa in the spring of 1942.

We still had our first Christmas together before he left. It was and continues to be my favorite Christmas.

"Thelma, I hope you understand why I have to fight for our country. I'll be back here before you know it.

We have the rest of our lives in front of us after I get home from the war."

Henry never made it back home. He was killed when his M4 Sherman tank drove over a land mine in 1943. He was in the Second Armored Division under the leadership of General George Patton.

I thought my life was over. Henry's death left me with such a void in my heart. I couldn't bear to lose anyone else in my life, but I did. Betsy Grace left us that year, too, and we didn't know where she went. Somehow, though, the sun comes up every morning and there's always hope for a better tomorrow.

Chapter 7
Lottie Reveals a Secret Hiding Place (Betsy Grace's Diary, 1931-1938)

"We know what it takes to have grit and we know what it means to never quit."
Lyrics from Southern Grit & Glamour

"Aunt Lottie, are you sure you're up to having us all at your house for the Christmas Holidays?" CJ asked.

"Of course I am. I wouldn't have it any other way," I replied.

Thelma and her crew were going to be here in a few days and I still hadn't done the grocery shopping. It was going to be so special to have everyone home for Christmas. I thought it only proper to invite

John Mark, too, since he is Austin's granddaddy and Ashley's great granddaddy. He even offered to have our Christmas dinner at the farm, but I told him I wanted us to be at our house.

Brother Mike was knocking on my door just as I was opening it to go to the store to stock up on everyone's favorite foods.

"Hello, Lottie. I heard through the grapevine that you're having a big family Christmas this year and I was wondering if I'm still considered part of the family," he smiled.

"Yes, I was going to stop by the church to see if you were around and invite you over for dinner after I finished at the grocery store. Thelma and her family will be here for Christmas Eve services," I said.

"Well, that's great. How would you like some help with the shopping?"

What a man Brother Mike is! He seems to always show up when you need him the most.

"I'd love it if you tagged along," I replied.

* * *

We not only went to the grocery store, we also stopped by Jean and Joe's Place to order apple, pecan, and pumpkin pies for our Christmas dinner.

Tallulah Belle was sitting inside sipping her morning coffee when we stepped inside. She turned her head and smiled as if she knew it was us coming in. She had difficulty seeing at 85 years of age, but somehow she recognized her friends every time one stopped in the cafe.

"Hi, Tallulah Belle. It sure is good to see you in here this morning. Don't tell me you've been back in the kitchen making pies since daybreak," I said.

"Now, Lottie Jean, you know that Christmas pies don't get made around here unless I'm in the kitchen supervising what's going on. This younger generation doesn't know what it takes to make the pies just right," she remarked.

"I'm glad you're seeing to the baking. We're here to order two of each kind." I told her.

"Good to hear. I was thinking about you and your family as I got dressed this morning. Do you remember the time Betsy Grace thought she would help me bake pies for Christmas? She was always in a hurry to get things done. I told her we had to take our time so that the pies came out just right, but she decided she knew how to take shortcuts with the recipes and baking time to get more pies ready for the customers.

I'll never forget Gertrude's mama storming in here after she picked up her pie order and demanded her money back. The good news is Gertrude sneaked a bite of the apple pie before they got home. She gagged and spit it out.

'My poor daughter almost threw up on her new white pinafore. I took a bite, too, and it was the worst taste of pie I've ever had in my life,' she told us."

Tallulah did her best recreation of Gertrude's mother she could muster.

"Not only did we not save time baking pies that Christmas, we had to throw away all of the apple pies and start over. Nevertheless, the Christmas pies of 1932 were saved because Gertrude Jones ate a piece of pie when she shouldn't have. Who would've thought?"

Tallulah Belle and I were laughing so hard we couldn't get our breath. I decided right then and there that I would tell CJ where to find Betsy Grace's diary in the attic and bring it down for us to read together. Betsy Grace always kept it in a hidden drawer in her vanity dresser. I knew she kept it there, but I never did get it out and read it even when she was alive. I liked knowing where she hid it and that was *my* secret.

Maybe there would be time after the others arrived for us to take turns reading her entries by the fireplace after supper. It was time the twins got to know a little bit about their grandmother.

* * *

Thelma and the rest of the family arrived shortly before sundown on December 22nd. We had Cara's and Ashley's favorites, taco salad and chocolate shakes to celebrate being together.

I walked over to the fireplace and took the diary off the mantle. I turned to face Thelma and asked, "Do you know what this is" as I handed it to her.

She looked at the cover for what seemed like an eternity and then she lifted her head and looked at me with tears in her eyes. "It's Betsy Grace's diary. Where did you find it?"

"I've had it all along. I used to sneak a peek at her whenever I knew she was writing in it and then watch her put it up for the night. She kept it in a hidden drawer in her vanity dresser. Don't you remember Mama buying that dresser for her 16th birthday?" I asked.

"Yes, I remember her getting it for her birthday, but I didn't know it had a hidden drawer. How did you know about that?" Thelma asked.

"She showed it to me right after the delivery man brought it to our house. The store manager told her about it when we went into Del Rio to look for her birthday present. I think you had gone into the candy store next door. You wanted to get Betsy candy for her birthday."

Mama never touched Daddy's savings except when we had birthdays. She thought birthdays should be special every year, so she would let us go into Del Rio on our birthdays to pick out our gifts. Normally, she wouldn't spend as much as she paid for the dresser, but she decided that on each of our 16th birthdays, we could pick out something extra special for our "Sweet Sixteen".

"Well, how about that. All this time I've been oblivious to that fact. Betsy Grace should have known that you would know that would be the perfect place to hide her diary." Thelma exclaimed.

"Part of me thinks she did know I was spying on her when she hid her diary, but I think she also knew that I wouldn't ever pry." I said.

"I'm glad we have her diary, Lottie. Thanks for waiting for us to get here to read it." Thelma said with more tears in her eyes.

"CJ, Cara, Ashley! Leave those dishes and come sit by the fire while we read something special together." I hollered.

Austin and Glen went over to see John Mark for a guys' night out which allowed us to have a girls' night in.

"I want us to take turns reading the passages. I'll start and then hand it to one of you next."

August 11, 1931

Today is my 16th birthday. It has been such a special day, not just because it's my birthday, but because I got to spend it with my mama and sisters. How blessed I am to have them in my life. Mama bought me a dresser with Daddy's savings that she keeps in the kitchen in a coffee can above the ice box. She shouldn't have spent so much on the dresser even though it is a used one, it still cost more than she usually spends on our birthdays. She said she wanted all of us to have a special "Sweet Sixteen" so tomorrow a man from the store in Del Rio will deliver it to our house.

Lottie gave me this diary and Thelma gave me a box of chocolates. As I sit here eating the chocolates and writing in my new diary I have to close by thanking God for all that we have, especially each other.

August 15, 1931

Mama looks so tired. I wish she didn't have to work two jobs. We try to bring in money, too, but there's never enough. I'm thinking about selling my new dresser to her best friend, Tallulah Belle. She came by the house to see it after Mama told her about it and loved it so much she said she wanted to get one just like it. I 'm going to stop writing tonight and go sing Mama the song I wrote today while ironing for the Avery's.

"What was the song Betsy Grace used to sing to Mama?" I asked.

"Don't you remember she sang:

'I know the Lord will listen, He listens every night and day. I love the Lord to listen. All I have to do is pray.'"

Thelma sang the chorus every bit as well as Betsy Grace used to sing it.

"That's it. How did you remember which song it was?" I asked.

"I remember all the songs she wrote and sang," Thelma replied.

"I wish I'd shown you the diary before now. We should have known something had to have happened to our sister. She would never have left Mama or Jean long term."

I put my head in my hands and sighed.

"It's okay, Lottie. You didn't know what was going through her head when she left Truway. You were angry and scared at the same time, after she moved away." Thelma walked over, knelt down, and put her arm around me.

"May I read some of her entries, Aunt Lottie?"
CJ asked.

I handed the diary to her.

December 22, 1932

*It's been so long since I've written, but I had to write
today. My sisters and I have been asked to sing in
another church outside of Truway. We've sung in our
church on several occasions and last Sunday, someone
from another country church heard us and asked us
to come to her church on Christmas Eve. The best
news yet is Mr. Chilacothe asked us sing in the next
Chilacothe Farms Festival this summer. We need to
decide on a name for our group. Most folks call us
"The Trinity Girls", but that just doesn't sound like a
singing group to me. We're so busy right now though
I can't think of a better name. Maybe something will
come to me later.*

"I remember when that happened. We were traveling
around the county singing every weekend." I declared.

June 10, 1933

*You won't believe what happened today. We met a girl
called Ray Nell and she not only will join our singing
group, she and Lottie were the inspirations for our new
name—Southern Grit & Glamour. Now that's a name!*

"Ray Nell was so funny. I wish she were still around to share some of these memories. She moved back to El Paso after you moved to New Mexico. It would be great to send her a card and let her know we appreciate all that she did while she was in Truway," Lottie said.

July 5, 1933

We were a hit. A record is just around the corner. John Mark Chilacothe played the saxophone for us and it really added a great sound to our songs. I can hardly wait for the next Summer Festival.

"Thelma, do you remember the first summer festival? Wasn't that the year you told everyone that you saw Bonnie and Clyde in Truway?" I asked.

"I will always remember our first performance as a group. It was magical, and yes, Tallulah Belle and I are convinced that Bonnie and Clyde drove through Truway and stopped long enough to eat at the diner and get Bonnie's hair fixed. Our mother washed and styled a notorious criminal's hair," Thelma said emphatically.

June 1, 1934

I can't believe it has almost been a whole year since I wrote in my diary. I actually left it in a trunk where we keep our performance dresses and didn't know it was there until we got the dresses out today to see which ones we want to wear this year for the Festival. My diary was laying at the bottom of the trunk just waiting for me to write in it again.

I met the cutest boy ever this morning. He's here visiting John Mark. He's tall, has sandy blond hair, blue eyes and chiseled cheek bones. My heart skipped a beat when he said "hello" to me.

"Hi there. What's your name?" he asked.

"My name is Betsy Grace Trinity. What's yours?"

"It's Tommy Earl Nelson. I'm staying at the Chilacothe's all summer. John Mark said he plays in your band. Do you think you might let me join your group, too?" he asked.

"What instrument do you play?" I asked this ever so handsome man.

"I can play the drums and I must say, I play them very well," he said.

"I'm sure you do, but we still have to ask you to audition. We don't just take someone's word for their musical talents." I said in what I hoped was an authoritative voice, but I'm sure he heard my voice shaking. My heart was beating so hard, I figured he heard that, too.

Tommy Earl played his drums for us and looked at me the entire time he was playing. I knew right then that

I was going to marry this man someday.

August 13, 1934

Today is my wedding day! Tommy Earl and I got married this morning at sunrise. He's such a wonderful husband already. He said he's going to bring me a cup of coffee every morning before he goes out to the fields. We're fortunate enough to live in one of the bunk houses on the farm.

It needs a woman's touch, but it will take time to fix it up to my liking. Money is tight for everyone. I'm working with Mama at the Truway Beauty Shop during the week and at Della's Diner on weekends. Work is okay and life is good.

December 20, 1934

I went to the doctor today because I've been unable to keep anything down for a week. What I thought was a stomach bug turned out to be a baby. I can't believe that Tommy Earl and I will be parents sometime in early June. Wait 'til he hears this news. I hope he'll be as excited as I am.

December 25, 1934

As soon as I woke up this morning I started a fire in the stove and made Tommy his favorite breakfast while he was out tending to the animals.

I heard Tommy coming in the front door just as I was putting the bacon on a plate.

"Betsy, why aren't you sleeping in on Christmas morning? I was going to make you breakfast in bed today," he said.

"This is one of my Christmas gifts to you. Your other present in sitting in your favorite chair."

I pretended I was busy finishing up breakfast as I watched him walk over to his chair and pick up his present. He shook it and said, "It's awfully light. Are you sure you remembered to put something in the box?" He teased.

I smiled at him, cocked my head to the side and said, "Just open it, okay? Your breakfast is almost done and I want you to open your present before we eat."

Tommy tore into the box and pulled out the tissue paper. "There's nothing here," he exclaimed.

"Look under the tissue paper at the bottom." He threw out the rest of the tissue paper and picked up the envelope inside. "What's this? Are you giving me money for Christmas? You don't need to give me money, Betsy. I would be happy with breakfast and a foot rub."

He opened the card and began reading. "I don't get it. Why do I need to wait for my Christmas present until June?"

"Keep reading, please," I said.

He started reading the rest out loud. "Your gift will be presented to you in June. You'll have to wait to see if it's a boy or girl, but I know it will be one or the other. Congratulations!"

"Are you trying to tell me we're going to have a baby?" he cried.

He threw the card down, ran over to me, picked me up and twirled me around. "I'm sorry. I hope I didn't make you sick," he said as he put my face between his hands and touched his nose to mine.

Instead of saying anything, I wrapped my arms around him and said, "I love you so much, Tommy Earl Nelson!"

June 5, 1935

Jean Louise Trinity Nelson was born in the wee hours this morning. She is the most beautiful baby I've ever seen! I can't even imagine life without her. It seems as if she has been with us always.

Her strawberry blond hair and blue eyes are her most intriguing features, but her smile causes everyone around her to smile, too. She is going to be a happy child and Tommy Earl and I are blessed beyond measure.

June 5, 1936

Our little Jean turned one today. My writing is surely sporadic, but I have my hands full taking care of my family and helping Mama when I can at the shop and the diner. Southern Grit & Glamour has been asked to perform at the Summer Festival. We didn't perform last year so I guess we'll take the time to rehearse two of our songs and give it a go. John Mark isn't here to play his saxophone, but we have the rest of the group and we'll be ready to give our best performance.

July 4, 1936

I can't believe what happened tonight at the festival. Just as we were about to get up on stage, we heard a cracking sound which caused us to stop and look around to see what was going on. Without warning, a big tree branch from one of the oldest oak trees on the farm came crashing down and landed right in the middle of the stage. Some of the limbs hit the back drop and it came tumbling down, too. The worst part is that Tommy Earl's drums were under the fallen tree.

It took all of us and several other people to clean off the stage. The drums were damaged so we decided we wouldn't try to perform this year. Maybe next year, but it will take time to earn money to buy a new drum set. Oh well, at least no one was hurt. For that we are thankful.

June 14, 1938

It has been almost two years since I wrote in this diary! Life has been so busy and I'm just too tired each night to write, but I wanted to write tonight. Tommy Earl is going up in a plane tomorrow. Mr. Chilacothe wants him to get his pilot's license and be his personal pilot when he needs to fly somewhere to promote the farm's vegetables. They also talked about implementing some fancy new crop dusting for the veggies. It scares me, but I know that Tommy wants to do this so much. I'll just keep busy with Jean and my day-to-day activities.

June 18, 1938

We buried Tommy Earl today. His plane went down three days ago. I can't believe he's gone. The love of my life is not here to bring me coffee in the morning. He won't be able to watch our little girl grow up. The pain is unbearable. I don't know if I'll have the strength to carry on without him, but I have to remember that Jean needs me and Tommy would want me to be strong for her sake. Thank you, God for the time I had with Jean's daddy. Take extra care of him in heaven until I get up there to see him again.

CJ stopped reading and looked up at us. We were all sobbing. She walked over to us and put her arms around Thelma and me. Cara and Ashley got up and came over to us, too, and put their arms around us and CJ. Eventually CJ walked over to the mantle and placed the diary on the top.

"I guess it's time for the Trinity girls to call it a night," CJ said.

Cara took Aunt Thelma by the hand and Ashley took me by the hand as we walked up the stairs to our rooms.

I turned and looked back at the fire in the fireplace. It was almost out, but the embers were still glowing as if to say, "everything's going to be okay."

I smiled at CJ and she smiled back and then followed us up the stairs.

December 25, 193_

As soon as I woke up this morning I started a fire in the stove and made Tommy his favorite breakfast while he was out tending to the animals.

I heard Tommy coming in the front door just as I was putting the ha__ _ plate.

"This is one of my Christmas gifts to you. Your other present is sitting in your favorite chair."

I pretended I was busy finishing up breakfast as I watched him w__k over to his chair and pi_ _ _ _ present. He shook t_ a_ _ _ _ _ _ _ pu_ _ _ to

COFFEE

Chapter 8
Thelma's Christmas Visit
(Betsy Graces' Diary,
1940-1943)

**"In every situation God gives me blessed consolation
that my trials come to only make me strong."
Lyrics from Through It All**

It's Christmas Eve in the year 2001 and we have
been cooking and decorating all day. The only
thing missing is the snow we'd have if we were at
the ranch. Maybe next year everyone can come up to
New Mexico for Christmas.

"Thelma, it's so good to have you here with me."
Lottie said.

"Thanks. I love being here, but was thinking about
asking you to have Christmas with me at the ranch
next year. What do you think about that plan?" I asked.

"It's a deal. I think we ought to trade off years for as long as we are able to travel. We're not spring chickens anymore, you know." Lottie laughed.

She was right. We are both in our eighty's now and not as spry as we once were. I walked over to the fireplace so that I could enjoy its warmth. My arthritic hands were ice cold and needed to warm up before we went to bed. Tomorrow was going to be a big day—presents, Brother Mike, and the rest of the family for Christmas dinner.

"Lottie, before we turn in for the evening do you want to read more from Betsy Grace's diary?" I asked.

"I didn't realize there were more entries. The last one was when she wrote about burying Tommy Earl." Lottie sighed.

"CJ told me there were other entries, but she knew we needed time before we continued reading," I said.

"Where are the girls? I want them with us if we're going to read the diary," Lottie said.

They went over to John Mark's with the guys to get more firewood for the fireplace, but they should be back any time." I replied.

Just then the front door opened and in walked our family. "We were hoping you'd return soon. We want to continue reading the diary if you're up to it." I said.

"Sure. Let us put on our pajamas and we'll be back to read more," Cara perked up.

"Glen, do you want to sit in here while we read or go into the kitchen to cut into one of the pecan pies we bought at Jean and Joe's Place?" Cara asked.

"That's a difficult decision to make, but I vote for pecan pie. How about you guys?" Glen looked over at Austin and Charlie Jay.

"Pecan pie it is." Austin remarked.

As the guys walked through the kitchen door, CJ, Cara, and Ashley were coming down the stairs dressed in their comfy pajamas.

"I'll start where we left off if it's okay with everyone else." I said. They nodded and smiled.

May 10, 1940

It's been almost two years since Tommy Earl left us. I didn't care to write anything until today. The most unusual thing happened today at Big Southern Hair Beauty Salon. A man from out of town walked in to see if we cut hair for men.

"Hello, do you have a barber in this salon?" He asked.

"Yes, we do," I replied. "She's with someone right now, but she could cut your hair in the next 30 minutes. Would you like a shave, too, or just the haircut?" I asked.

"A shave sounds great. My name is Tom Frank

Buchanan. I'm passing through on my way to Mexico. We're hosting a musical festival in Mexico City. We're staying the night in Del Rio before heading out tomorrow, but decided to take a day trip to Truway," Mr. Buchanan said.

"My name is Betsy Grace. My mama owns the salon and I work here, too," I said.

"We were eating dinner at our hotel last night and we met some folks from Truway. We got to talking and they said we needed to drive over here and visit the Chilacothe Farms vegetable stand. They told us the vegetables with thyme were extraordinary. Of course, we can't take anything with us to Mexico, but we thought we would check out the stand and see if we want to extend our trip and come back through here on our way back to Del Rio."

"They are becoming more and more popular. I think you'll want to take some home with you when you return from your trip." I said.

"What do you do for fun in Truway, Betsy Grace?" He asked suddenly.

"W-W-Well I spend most of my free time with my daughter, Jean." I replied.

"Oh, shoot. I knew it was too good to be true for you to be single," he said as he pushed his hat back on his head.

"I'm a widow. My husband died two years ago," I said weakly.

"I'm so sorry. What happened to him if you don't mind me asking," he inquired.

"He was in Mr. Chilacothe's plane getting in some flying time. He planned to be Mr Chilacothe's personal pilot, but something went wrong and his plane crashed into one of the fields." I was able to get the words out, but I don't know how. It felt like I was choking on them.

"I'm sure spending time with your precious daughter is a delight indeed," he replied.

I nodded and then noticed it was his turn to get his hair cut and shave. "Bobbie Jo is ready for you now. It was nice talking with you and I hope you have a good trip to Mexico." I said as I stood to show him where to go.

After Mr. Buchanan left I watched him go over to Della's Diner apparently to get something to eat. I was scheduled to take Tallulah Belle's place at the diner at two today. She needed to take off for a few hours. I wonder if he'll ask her what she does for fun in Truway, too.

June 3, 1940

I was working in the diner when I heard someone call out to me. "Betsy Grace, what are you doing in here?

I thought you worked in the salon." I turned and saw Tom Frank Buchanan smiling at me from the doorway.

"I work here, too, on weekends. How was Mexico?" I asked as I took him to a table.

"It was a good trip. We're thinking about bringing one of the singers we met at the festival to Nashville to cut a record," he said.

"I didn't know you lived in Nashville." I said.

"I never got around to telling you where I was from the last time I came through Truway. I am taking your advice and going back out to Chilacothe Farms so that I can get some of those famous vegetables to take home," he said as he opened the menu. "What do you recommend I order?"

"Today's special is meatloaf, but I'm partial to the chicken and dumplings," I pointed to the place where they were listed on the menu.

"Chicken and dumplings it is," he closed the menu and handed it back to me.

"As I walked back to the kitchen Tallulah Belle intercepted me and said, "Do you know who that is?"

"Yes, his name is Tom Frank Buchanan," I replied.

"He's a well-known music agent from Nashville." Tallulah Belle gushed.

"How do you know he's well-known?" I asked.

"He told me he was the last time he was in here to eat," she said indignantly.

"Did he ask you what you do for fun in Truway when he was in here last?" I laughed.

"No, but he asked if we had anyone in town who ever became famous and I told him, 'no', but we had a great musical group once."

"What musical group?" I asked.

"Southern Grit & Glamour, of course. You know you were the best we've ever had in Truway or in all of Buford County for that matter," she grinned.

"Thank you, Tallulah. I appreciate you saying that. It means a lot to know there are folks who liked hearing us sing," I said.

"You ought to tell him that you're from Southern Grit & Glamour. It would be great if you and the rest of the group performed for him while he's in town. You never know, he just might want to take you to Nashville to make a record," Tallulah said excitedly.

"I couldn't ask him to take time to listen to us, Tallulah, but it's nice of you to think we're good enough to make a record," I smiled at her as I turned in the "famous" music agent's order.

"Will there be anything else, Mr. Buchanan?" I asked after I cleared his dishes from the table.

"Yes, there is, Betsy Grace." His smile was wolfish, but handsome, "Would you be kind enough to set a time when I can hear you and the rest of Southern Grit & Glamour. I love the name!

Please tell me it was your invention." He grinned.

"How did you know that I am a member of Southern Grit & Glamour?" I asked.

"Your friend, Tallulah came over while you had your back turned and told me that you were the lead singer. Is that true?" He asked.

"You mean 'former friend,'" I shot a look over my shoulder at Tallulah that would melt wax and she smiled and waved at me. "I am or I mean I was." I turned back to Tom Frank.

"We haven't sung in a long time. My sisters and a good friend were also in the band. We don't have a drummer and saxophone player any more so I don't know how we'd sound," I replied.

"I would still be honored to hear you sing. How about it?" He asked.

"There's a back room here for parties and family reunions. I guess Della would let us use it tonight if you really want to hear us," I said.

"How about seven o'clock?" He asked as he stood, tipped his hat, and started walking away, leaving me no chance to rebuff him.

"Thank you, Mr. Buchanan." I called out to him. He turned and looked at me, smiled, and said," Betsy Grace, please quit calling me 'Mr. Buchanan'. My name is Tom. See you at seven," And he walked out of the diner.

* * *

CJ interrupted me. "Is that when you made the record we listened to at the ranch?"

"Yes. We didn't go to Nashville to make the record, but Tom Frank knew people in Del Rio who set up the recording to cut the album. We showed up that evening to sing for him. Do you remember that night, Lottie?" I asked.

"Yes, I remember that night. I also remember telling you after we left the diner that I didn't trust him as far as I could throw him. Do you remember me telling you that?" Lottie glared.

"Tom Frank Buchanan fell in love with our sister and that's why you didn't like him. You didn't want him to take her away from us," I said.

"I never liked him because he had shifty eyes. It's not like he wanted to marry her and raise Jean. He wanted to exploit her in my opinion. I bet you anything that he had something to do with her death. I think we need to find out where he is today, if he's still alive, and ask him what happened to our sister," Lottie's face turned red with anger.

"May I read now?" Cara asked.

"Please do," I said as I handed the diary to her.

June 5, 1940

It's Jean's fifth birthday. She got up at the crack of dawn and jumped up and down beside my bed. "Get up, Mommy. It's time to have my birthday party."

"Okay, little princess. Let's get up and wake everyone else for our favorite pancake breakfast," I said as she pulled on my arm. She drug me out the door and down the stairs at break-neck speed.

As we approached the kitchen I heard a knock on our front door. Mama was already in the kitchen so Jean ran to her telling her how many pancakes she planned to eat while I turned to see who was at the door.

I cracked it open and saw Tom Frank Buchanan on our threshold. "Good morning, Betsy. I realize it's very early in the morning, but I had to come over to tell you 'thank you for allowing me to visit once again and get the opportunity to listen to your amazing voice. I also came to say 'so long for now, but not goodbye'," he said.

"Hello, Tom. Please come in for a cup of coffee and Mama's famous pancakes before you head out of town," I said as I stepped aside to let him enter.

"Coffee will be great, but I don't have time for pancakes today. May I take you up on the breakfast offer when I return?" He asked.

"Sure. We'll go into the kitchen to pour your coffee. You said you'll be back. When do you expect to return to Truway?" I asked.

"If I play my cards right, I'll be back in a few months. I'm going to take the recording you and the girls did to Nashville and play it for a record producer I know. He's going to love the way you sound. If he likes it as much as I think he will I'm going to come back to ask you to accompany me to Nashville to record your songs for him in his studio. What do you think about that?" He grinned from ear to ear.

"Oh, my. I had no idea you liked our songs so much. We can't afford to travel to Nashville, Tom, but I appreciate your confidence in Southern Grit & Glamour." I replied.

He stared at me for a moment with a smile on his face

and then he pulled a little box out of his pocket and handed it to me. I opened the box and saw a beautiful ruby ring inside.

"Is this for me?" I asked.

"Yes, it is. I bought it for you because it reminds me of a glowing ember and that's what I think about when I hear you sing," he said. I took the ring out and looked at the stone and then studied the inside of the band. It said, "To BGT. From TFB.

"Thanks, Tom. It's beautiful. I don't feel right accepting such an expensive gift," I told him.

"I can't take it back now. It's engraved with our initials. Please wear it and think of me. Please, don't worry about the expenses, Betsy. The production company will pay for your travel," he also said as he looked at his watch.

"That's exciting. It sounds too good to be true, if I'm honest, but we look forward to discussing the possibility further when you return," I said.

"It's later than I thought. I'll have to wait on that coffee for another time, too," he said as he turned and hurried out the door, leaving me confused and clutching the ring.

Before Cara got to the next entry about Tom Frank's next visit, Lottie interrupted her and said, "I don't think I want to hear the next part, Cara. Tom Frank Buchanan's next visit wasn't pleasant," she emphasized.

"It wasn't pleasant for us, but it was for Betsy Grace," I spoke up.

"What happened when he came back?" CJ asked.

"Cara, go ahead and read what happened next. Lottie, if you don't want to hear it, you can go upstairs," I said.

Lottie got up and started to the stairs, but then turned and came back and sat down with a huff.

"I guess I'll need to hear it from Betsy's perspective rather than hold on to my own bitter memories," she said.

Cara continued reading.

July 5, 1941

We decided to sing in the Chilacothe Summer Festival. Times were getting better. The depression is over. People were happy and glad to celebrate new beginnings. I'd never seen so many people at the festival ever. Not only did others from Buford County attend this year, but we saw many new faces in the crowd. I hadn't seen Tom Frank Buchanan in over a year so I was surprised to see him in the audience with some other fellow when we sang our signature song to a standing ovation. After it was over he walked up to the stage and introduced me to his friend. "Betsy, this is Saul Baker, the music producer I told you about last year," he said.

"Hello, Betsy. You sound even better in person. I'm honored to meet you," he said as he extended his hand to shake mine.

"Thank you, Mr. Baker. We appreciate your kind words. Please meet the rest of the group. This is Lottie, Thelma, Ray Nell, and our newest member, Tallulah Belle," I said as they each curtsied when I said their names.

"Betsy, do you think we could go over to that picnic table and talk a little business?" Mr. Baker asked.

"Let me talk with my sisters and friends about their evening plans first," I replied.

"Betsy, the rest of your group can go ahead with their evening. We'll talk with you and then you can relay the information to the others later," Tom Frank interjected.

"That's exactly how it happened. As soon as I heard Tom Frank tell Betsy that the rest of us weren't needed in the business talk, I knew something fishy was up. Mr. Buchanan always smelled fishy to me and it broke my heart that Betsy couldn't see him for what he truly was," Lottie interrupted Cara again.

"Lottie, I know it hurt when you realized that they didn't want all of us to go to Nashville. It hurt my feelings, too, but Betsy was trying to honor us and at the same time think about her musical future," I said.

"Her future was to stay put in Truway with her family. She had her daughter to raise. She had us. Mama was starting to falter that very night. Do you remember how we had to take Mama home right away and not get to stay at the festival?" Lottie asked.

"Yes, I remember how you caught her just before she fell when we were walking over to get corn-on-the-cob," I nodded.

"What happened next?" CJ asked.

"Mama's heart was giving out, but we didn't realize just how much until a few years later," I said.

"I will always believe that Mama's heart was breaking right before our eyes when she realized Betsy was going to leave and go to Nashville with Tom Frank Buchanan," Lottie exclaimed.

"Cara, may I read now?" I asked.

"Of course, Aunt Thelma," she said.

I took the diary from her and scanned the next entry briefly before I read what happened next.

September 7, 1941

Mama was in the hospital for few days in August so I haven't had time to think about Tom Frank or

Nashville. Mama needed us all to pick up the pace while she was mending. I got a letter from Tom Frank, but haven't even had time to open it until today. We've been planning Thelma's wedding to Henry Tune.

Betsy Grace,

I haven't heard from you in a while so I thought I would write to see what's going on. I'm hoping you are trying to get your life in order so that you can come to Nashville. If there's a reason why you can't come now, please let me know so that I can let Saul know. He's scheduled your recording for December 16th. Can you tell me if that date is okay with you?

Sincerely,

Tom Frank

I wrote Tom and told him about Mama's illness and Thelma's wedding. He wrote back and said he was disappointed to postpone the recording, but he'd be glad to reschedule it for some time in the spring when Mama got her strength back and things settled down.

April 7, 1942

It has been like a whirlwind around here in the last few months. Thelma moved to Henry's ranch in a place called Whistle Stop, New Mexico in the fall. We've been working twelve hour shifts.

Running the salon for Mama has been very time consuming and the diner was always full. I heard from Tom Frank again last month. He said that Saul Baker would have to forego my opportunity to record unless I could come to Nashville within the next year. I talked with Mama about it. She told me she would support any decision I made. If I went to Nashville this summer, I'd have to leave Jean with Mama and Lottie. When I tried to talk to Lottie about going, she wouldn't talk to me. She walked away from me every time I started a conversation with her. I guess I'll have to write her a letter before visiting Thelma in New Mexico. My hope is that she'll realize it's only for a short while. I'll be back home as soon as I record a few songs.

July 5, 1942

We didn't sing in the festival this summer. Lottie is still not speaking to me and Thelma couldn't break away from the ranch to sing with us, so we just stayed home and listened to the sounds of the festival from our front porch. Jean and I are planning to spend the rest of the summer and part of the fall with Thelma since Henry went off to war.

I stopped reading and silently read the next entry. It was a special entry meant just for Lottie and I didn't want to read it out loud.

"Why did you stop reading, Thelma?" Lottie asked.

"The next entry is to you and I don't feel right reading it to everyone. That will have to be your decision," I said as I handed the diary to her with tears in my eyes.

She stared at the page for just a fraction of a second and then she continued reading.

July 10, 1942

Lottie,

I've seen you watch me as I write in my diary and then pretend you don't see where I put it when I am finished writing. My hope is that once I'm gone to New Mexico, you'll find this letter I've written to you in my diary. I love you more than words can say. It hurts so much to see you angry with me. You're so strong-willed and that's a trait I've always admired in you, but right now it's getting in the way of our love for each other. I know you love me and want the best for me, but I have to do what I think is right for Jean and me. Please search your heart and remember how we've always had each other's backs. I love you, Lottie Jean Trinity, and I will return to Truway soon.

Love Your sister,

Betsy Grace

Lottie laid the diary down beside her and before she could look up, I was sitting on her other side, putting my arms around her neck and holding her while she wept on my shoulder.

* * *

That was the last entry in the diary. Lottie hadn't read her final letter to her until last night. After Lottie composed herself, she looked at me and said, "Thelma, whatever it takes, we will find out where Tom Frank Buchanan is and get him to tell us what he knows about Betsy Grace's death. Promise me you'll help me search for him," she said.

"I promise," I replied. Lottie never trusted Tom Frank. I don't know if he is responsible for our sister's death, but Lottie was right. We needed to find him and ask him questions about his last night with Betsy Grace

Chapter 9
On the Road to Nashville
(Lottie, 2002)

*"Just give me the strength to do every day
what I have to do."*
Lyrics from One Day at a Time

Mount Hope cemetery is such a beautiful place. It's a place where memories live even though there's scarce a sound to be heard. On this particular day I hear a Mourning Dove in the tree above where we buried Daddy, Mama, Tommy Earl, Betsy Grace, and Jean. I haven't visited since we laid Betsy Grace to rest, if only technically, I don't feel she will be totally laid to rest until we find out what happened in 1943.

After I put flowers on all their graves, I stepped back, sighed, and said, "Mama, I hope you know we finally found your oldest daughter and that she is lying beside you, Tommy Earl, and her baby girl."

"Betsy, thank you for writing to me before you left for New Mexico. I'm just sorry that I didn't read what you had to say when you left Truway. I pledge to you that we'll find out what happened to you. We love you and miss you as much today as the day you left us."

Wallking back to John Mark's truck I saw a butterfly fluttering past, an example of the vibrancy of spring and a hope for a better tomorrow.

* * *

"Aunt Lottie, Austin found that record company you asked him to look up. It's called, "Baker's Beats" and it's in the heart of Nashville close to Vanderbilt University." CJ called to me from the front room of her house. I was in the kitchen making our favorite taco salad for supper.

"That's wonderful. Ashley checked on the flights out of Del Rio and we can leave as early as tomorrow if that's okay with you and Austin." I said.

"We're fine with her going with you. We certainly don't want you going by yourself. It's too bad that Thelma fell off her horse and broke her hip. She wanted so much to travel with you." CJ replied.

I received a letter from Thelma three days ago
describing what happened to her while riding Betsy Too.

March 5, 2002

Dear Lottie,

*You won't believe what happened to me over the
weekend. I decided to ride out to No Man's Gulch
and look around in the cave where we found Betsy's
remains. Ashley mentioned an old boot being beside
the gravel pile, but I don't remember her bringing it
back to the ranch with the ring so I went out there to
see if the boot was still in the cave.*

*The good news is that it was and I tied it to my saddle
to bring home so I could get a better look at it. I was
almost back in view of the ranch when a rattlesnake
spooked Betsy, Too. She reared up and when she did,
I slid off the back of the saddle and onto the rocky
ground. My first thought was to see where the snake
was, but when I tried to move, I couldn't. I knew
something was broken and I'd have to wait for someone
to come look for me. When I surveyed my surroundings,
I saw Sam.*

*He ran over to me and just stood there as if to say, "I'm
here to protect you." Behind him I saw Charlie Jay
running toward me. "Thelma, what happened? Betsy,
Too just showed up in the barn without you. Did she
throw you?"*

"A rattlesnake spooked her and when she reared up, I fell off her. I think I've broken something because I can't move."

Charlie told Sam to stay with me and he went to get Juan.

I am now in the Whistle Stop Hospital waiting for the doctor to release me to go home. My hip is broken, but not my spirit. That's not the bad news though. I'm sad that I can't go with you to Nashville. I promised I'd be by your side. Please forgive me.

I look forward to hearing what you find out.

Until then, love from the ranch!

Thelma

Poor Thelma. This is the second time she has broken a bone while riding a horse. She's so tough and I am a little afraid to take this journey without her. She's the youngest, but has always had such inner strength. You'd think she was the oldest. I admire her attitude about life and hope to be more like her once I get some answers about Betsy Grace's demise.

* * *

"You can open your eyes now, Aunt Lottie. We're in the air and I trust the pilot to get us safely to Nashville." Ashley smiled at me from her window seat.

She gave me the opportunity to sit by the window, but I chose the aisle seat just in case I had to make a quick exit to the bathroom. I've never flown before and really didn't care to ever fly, but the drive would have been too long.

We traveled during Ashley's spring break so our time in Nashville was limited.

"Ashley, I'm fine now that we're in the air. I think I'll snooze a bit so that we can hit the road after checking into our hotel. I want to go to Baker's Beats today and see Saul Baker if he's still alive. He's our only hope in finding Tom Frank Buchanan." I said.

"I understand. We'll go there and see who's running the place. I'm sure you'll get some answers so that we can decide what to do next." Ashley patted my leg.

I leaned back, closed my eyes again, and could hear Betsy Grace singing in my ear, *"I know the Lord will listen, He listens every day. I know my Lord will listen, all I have to do is pray."*

I prayed that God would lead us to discover what happened to my sister and Ashley's great grandmother.

* * *

"Here we are." Ashley said as she pulled up in front of the record store. The once famous recording studio had been turned into a place to find and buy old records.

We walked in and heard a man ask, "May I help you find something?"

"Yes, we're looking for Saul Baker. Is he here?" I asked.

"I'm sorry to say that Saul Baker died five years ago. I'm his son, Sid. I'd be glad to help you." A man who resembled Saul said.

"Actually, we're looking for someone Saul used to know. His name is Tom Frank Buchanan. Did he ever mention that name to you?" I asked.

"As a matter of fact, he did. He used to tell me all kinds of stories about his adventures with Tom Frank." Sid replied.

"Is he still alive and if he is, do you know where he is?" Ashley asked.

"The last I heard, he was doing time in the Tennessee State Prison for embezzlement." Sid said.

Embezzlement! I knew Tom Frank Buchanan was a louse. "How long ago was that?" I asked.

"Gosh, I really don't remember how long ago it was. It was many years before my dad passed away because I remember Dad telling me the story when I was quite young. It seems that Tom Frank had promised a group of musicians that he'd represent them and make them stars. They paid him a hefty sum of money, but instead of investing the money in a record deal, he took off to Las Vegas and gambled all of the money away."

Sid chuckled, but then when he saw the look on my face, he became serious.

"I'm sorry. Did something like that happen to you, too?" He asked.

"No, it's worse. We believe he's the last person to see my sister alive and we want to question him about her death." I blurted.

Before Sid Baker excused himself to go help another couple who walked into the store, he looked at me and said, "I'm so sorry. I hope you get the answers you're looking for."

We left Baker's Beats and decided to return to our hotel so that we could locate the address of the state penitentiary.

* * *

"I called home and told Mom and Dad what we've discovered so far. They send their love and said they hope Tom Frank is still alive so that we can interview him." Ashley said as I came out of the bathroom.

The hot shower was wonderful and even though I tried to tell myself I wasn't ready for bed, my body said otherwise. "Thank you for being here with me, Ashley. It means a lot. Tomorrow will be another busy day, but we'll do it together. Sleep tight." I said.

* * *

The drive to the state prison was depressing. Seeing all the barbed wire at the top of the fence along the road makes me realize that there's still a lot to do in this world, but it's nice to know we all have a chance to change our destinies.

The guard at the entrance asked our names and checked our identification before allowing us to enter the front gates. After we parked and walked into a main entrance, we were asked to empty our pockets and walk through security. It was identical to what we had to go through to get on the plane to fly here.

After we passed through security we were asked to wait for an officer to come get us and take us to the area where we would be able to talk with Tom Frank Buchanan. The officer led us to an open room with several tables and chairs.

Yes, we found out Tom Frank was still alive! I'll never forget the thudding of my heart as I heard the guards say he was indeed one of their "residents". He had been there for over 10 years, but was not eligible for parole in the near future. We found out that he was convicted for two different embezzlement cases involving close to a million dollars; therefore, he was sentenced to 25 years in prison. I tried to remember what he looked like almost sixty years ago, but he would obviously look different now due to his age and his life behind bars.

Ashley put her arm through mine as we sat down and waited to meet Tom Frank Buchanan face-to-face.

We heard a sound like a door being unlocked and looked up to see an old man walking toward us. He peered at Ashley and then locked his eyes on me. I watched as recognition set in and it was apparent that he felt some sort of guilt upon seeing me again.

"Hello, Tom Frank," I said.

"You're Lottie, right? I remember those crystal clear blue eyes." He remarked as he took a chair across the table.

"Yes, good memory. I'm Lottie Trinity, Betsy Grace's sister," I replied.

"Why are you here?" He asked.

"We're here to find out what happened to my sister. This young lady beside me is her great granddaughter, Ashley." I tried to keep my voice steady.

Tom Frank nodded to Ashley and then said, "I don't know what you mean. I haven't seen Betsy Grace in almost sixty years." He said as he broke eye contact with me.

"You were the last person to see her!" I spoke too loudly. Other people visiting prisoners turned to see what was going on.

"I never got to see her. We were supposed to meet at the ranch, but when I arrived at the place she told me to meet her, she wasn't there. I waited for what seemed like an hour, but she never showed. I figured she changed her mind about going with me to Nashville, so I got back in my car and drove to Santa Fe. I flew home the next morning never to hear from her again." He said emphatically.

"I don't believe you!" I said again too loudly.

"I swear to you, Lottie. I don't know what happened to Betsy. I loved her. I would never hurt her in any way," he cried.

"If you loved her why didn't you try to find out why she didn't show up to meet you? You said you just left never to hear from her again. Didn't you wonder what happened to her? Weren't you concerned about not hearing from her if you loved her?" I was shouting at him.

Tom Frank didn't answer me. He slowly got up and then asked the guard to take him back to his cell.

I watched him walk away through the door the guard opened for him. He never looked back.

* * *

"I know you probably don't have much of an appetite, but I made us a reservation at *The Listening Room* downtown. They serve food and unknown musical talent line the stage to sing their songs with hopes of being 'discovered'." Ashley informed me when we returned to the hotel.

"I don't know Ashley. I'm frustrated, confused, and just plumb worn out." I said.

"Please go with me, Aunt Lottie. You have to eat something, sometime. We'll listen to a few of the artists and then return to our hotel room. It'll do you good to get out for a while." Ashley pleaded.

* * *

We arrived early so that we could get a seat close to the stage. We ordered our food and sat back and watched the other folks coming in. As I studied the people in the room I noticed someone familiar sitting by the stage entrance.

"Ashley, isn't that Sid Baker sitting over to our right?" I asked.

Ashley stood up to get a better look, "Yep, that's him. Do you think we should say, 'hello'?"

"No, he's too far away and it's not like we're friends with him. If he should walk by our table for any reason we can say something." I said.

The singers piled onto the stage just as our Nashville taco salads arrived along with the chocolate milkshakes we ordered for dessert.

There were three guys and three girls. They each took turns singing songs that they wrote themselves. We listened to five of them sing, but as the last singer introduced her song, my heart stopped beating for a second.

"Ashley, what did she say her song is called?" I asked not believing what I heard.

"She said, 'Southern Grit & Glamour', Aunt Lottie. Isn't that the name of the song Betsy Grace wrote?"

"It is. That couldn't be a coincidence, could it?" I asked still shocked at what I heard her say.

Before Ashley could answer, the young lady began singing,

"We know what it takes to have grit and we know what it means to never quit."

Before I heard anymore, I jumped up and walked quickly to where I saw Sid Baker sitting.

"Mr. Baker, may I have a word with you?" I asked.

"I'm sorry. Do I know you?" He asked me.

"We met today. I was in your store asking you about Tom Frank Buchanan. Do you remember me?"

"Oh, I remember you now. I can't talk to you right now. That's my daughter singing her new song. Can it wait until she's finished?" He asked tentatively.

I didn't know what to say, so I just sat there and waited for the song to be over. It was painful, yet enjoyable at the same time. His daughter's voice was amazing and I know Betsy Grace would have loved to hear her song sung by a talented musician from Nashville.

After she finished singing, the crowd in the room stood up and cheered for her performance.

"The singers will take a break so we have a few minutes to talk if you'd like." Sid Baker smiled.

We went out to the front porch and found some rocking chairs to sit in. I just stared at him for a minute so that I could gather my thoughts. I didn't want to come across in an accusing manner.

"Mr. Baker," I started.

"Please call me Sid. Did you find Tom Frank Buchanan?" He asked.

"Yes, we did. Thank you." I began again.

"Before we start, may I ask you what you thought about my daughter's song?" He asked.

"That's what I want to talk to you about, Sid." I said hesitantly.

"Really? You came over to the table before she finished singing. It's almost like you knew what she was going to sing," he chuckled, but then stopped when he saw the look on my face.

"Did your daughter say she wrote the song?" I asked.

"No, I know she didn't write it. My dad bought it from an agent years ago before he passed away. I found it about a year ago when I was cleaning out the back room at the store," he explained.

"Mr. Baker. I mean, Sid, did he buy it from Tom Frank by chance?" I asked.

"I'm not sure. He told me about this song and others he'd purchased for musicians back when the store was a recording studio, but like I said, I didn't find it until recently. My daughter has been writing her own songs, but when I showed her this one, she immediately decided she wanted to sing it tonight," he said.

Before I could say anything, he continued, "Have you heard the song before tonight?"

"Yes, I heard it right after my sister wrote it in 1934," I managed to say.

"Oh my goodness. Your sister wrote that incredible song? How come no one's heard it until now? Where's your sister now?" He asked turning beet red in the face.

"She's in the Mount Hope cemetery in Truway, Texas. We came here to question Mr. Buchanan about her death." I told him.

"Wow, I'm so sorry. Do you think my dad knew about the song?" He asked.

"He knew. We met your dad in 1941. He came to Truway and watched us perform in the Chilacothe Summer Festival. He wanted my sister to come to Nashville and record this song and others she wrote. We have a recording that was made in Del Rio prior to meeting your dad." I explained.

"Dad, it's time for us to get back on stage. Are you coming to hear my next song?" His daughter interrupted us.

"Yes, Harmony. I'm coming. You go on and I'll see you inside."

"I don't know what to say. Did Tom Frank have something to do with your sister's death?" He asked.

"He told us 'no', but I don't know whether to believe him or not." I replied.

"I know he's a scoundrel, but I can't see him killing anyone, but you know what, I want to go with you to see Mr. Buchanan one more time so that we can find out why he and my dad had your sister's song." He stood up and started to walk away and then turned and said, "I promise you that we will make sure your sister gets credit for writing her song. I'll pick you up at your hotel in the morning at eight o'clock. Where are you staying?" He asked.

I gave him the name of our hotel and then went to find Ashley. "We need to go get some rest now. Tomorrow promises to be another busy day. Call your parents and tell them we won't be home for a couple of days. The mystery just got more cryptic."

* * *

We are on our way back to the prison to see Tom Frank to not only question him again about the last time he saw Betsy Grace, but to also ask him why he sold her song to Saul Baker. Before we left I called Thelma and woke her up. I told her what I knew and wasn't surprised to hear her gasp, "You're kidding, right? You actually listened to a young woman sing *Southern Grit & Glamour*?"

"I'm not kidding. Ashley and I heard it with our own ears. I must say Harmony-that's her name-sang it beautifully." I said.

"Lottie, when you go see Tom Frank ask him what size boot he wears." Thelma said.

"Why would you want to know what size he wears? Are you talking about the boot you found in the cave?" I asked.

"It looks like a man's boot, size ten. We were able to see the size on the inside. I've sent it to the authorities in Santa Fe. You know that were in that cave and could have taken the boot to see if they could lift finger prints, but I remember them telling me back before we buried Betsy that there wasn't enough evidence to open a case. I disagree. I think that boot will help us find who was with Betsy when she died. If it's not Tom Frank's, we're back at square one." Thelma said.

* * *

We were surprised that Tom Frank agreed to see us. Of course we didn't tell him Ashley and I were with Sid. He came to talk to Sid, not us.

"Mr. Buchanan, I know that my dad liked you and I want to believe there's good in your heart somewhere. It's time for you to come clean. Why did you sell *Southern Grit & Glamour* when it wasn't yours to sell?"

"I didn't sell it right away. When I never heard from Betsy Grace again, I decided I needed some cash so I went to Saul and sold him the song so I could get out of trouble with some bad people. I think it's ironic that your dad never let anyone sing it before he died. Maybe he thought he'd hear from Betsy Grace and she'd still get the opportunity to sing her song in Nashville," he cried.

"Maybe you're right about Saul, but I know what *you* did was wrong and I still think you had something to do with my sister's death. By the way, what size shoe do you wear and are you missing an old boot?" I exploded.

"I wear a size thirteen and a half, why?" He said with tears streaming down his face.

Instead of answering him, I stood up, walked out to the car, and waited for Ashley and Sid.

* * *

We're on our way home. Before we left the prison we asked the guards what size shoe Tom Frank wore just in case he was lying to us. At least he told us the truth about his shoe size. So if the boot didn't belong to him, whose boot was left in the cave beside Betsy?

Our quest wasn't over yet.

Chapter 10
Celebrating Victory Bound
(Thelma, 2007-2015)

"Gratitude comes from the heart and once shared, it never departs."
Lyrics from A Grateful Heart

It's a beautiful day on the Las Bonitas ranch. Even though it's only seven in the morning, I hear joyous voices coming from Victory Bound campground. Today marks the camp's 25th Anniversary. The campers and counselors are getting ready for the annual end-of-camp show that they put on each summer, but this year it's going to be extra special. For some reason, I have kept out of the loop on the theme for this year's show. It will be fun to see what they have planned.

As I make my way to the swing on my front porch, I hear someone calling my name,

"Thelma, look at you walking outside without your walker. You are one tough lady," Charlie Jay remarked.

"I'm not only tough, I make the best pancakes in the state of New Mexico. Do you want to try some this morning before you get too busy with the campground festivities?" I asked.

"How can I pass up an opportunity to eat your blueberry pancakes?" He replied.

We turned to go into the house when I heard Cara calling out to Charlie Jay,

"Charlie, you're not going to believe what we just discovered! Our campground thief struck again. This time he not only took what food was left in the refrigerator, he cleaned out the kitchen cabinets and took our cooking supplies." She said exasperated.

"You're kidding. I was on guard last night. I never heard a sound coming from the kitchen area." Charlie Jay said.

"Didn't you go to bed around midnight and didn't one of the counselors volunteer to take the watch after you?" She asked.

"Justin took my place, but I remember him telling me this morning that his alarm didn't go off so he didn't get up to relieve me right away. He got out there closer to one. The thief must have taken everything between twelve and one," he replied.

"Glen called the sheriff. He'll be here soon to see if maybe this time the bandit left incriminating evidence." Cara turned and walked back to the campground.

"Thelma, as much as I want to eat your blueberry pancakes, I'll need to go back to camp and wait to see what the sheriff finds out about our mystery guest," Charlie Jay said.

I liked the idea of calling the burglar "our mystery guest". As much as I wanted us to catch this slippery fellow, I couldn't help but feel sorry for him or her. Obviously this person needed what was being taken.

* * *

Instead of making pancakes, I decided to make an assortment of sandwiches and ask someone to take them down to the campground dining area. The traditional hotdogs and all the fixings were in my refrigerator so the last night campfire celebration would prevail, but the campers needed something to eat during the day. With no food and no cooking supplies, the campers needed my help.

Charlie Jay returned to the house to give me an update on the campground theft and also to let me know he would be taking the campers on an orienteering adventure.

He walked into the house and called out my name. "Charlie, I'm in the kitchen." He sauntered into the kitchen with a bewildered look on his face.

"Thelma, I truly believe this is a day we won't soon forget. I promised the campers we would participate in the orienteering activity today. We've been working on it for over a week so I'll take them out to have fun with a "scavenger hunt" while Cara, Glen, and Ashley stay behind to visit with the sheriff about the last heist," he chuckled.

"Would you to take these sandwiches and jug of lemonade to the camp? But first you must tell me what orienteering is," I asked.

"Orienteering is a sport in which the campers find their way to various checkpoints across the ranch and beyond with only a map and a compass. Once they reach all checkpoints, there's a note on the last orange and white checkpoint flag that the first group to finish the course returns to me at the starting point. We heard about it last year from one of our campers and decided we'd give it a try this summer."

"Sounds like fun. I look forward to hearing about the winners and the content of the note when you get back. Please ask Cara to let me know what the sheriff says and how we plan to intercept the Victory Bound perpetrator," I said as I walked Charlie Jay to the door.

I went back to my porch swing with a hope that this time I could sit down and have quiet time between the Lord and me. "God, please keep everyone safe today and guide us with your everlasting wisdom. Amen."

* * *

"Aunt Thelma, are you okay?" Cara asked.

I jumped when I heard my name. "I must have dozed off. What time is it?"

"It's almost nine o'clock. I came to let you know what we know about our thief, but I also wondered if you've seen Sam this morning," Cara said.

"No, I haven't left the house and he hasn't come by to wish me well this morning like he usually does. Did you check to see if he's out by Ollie's grave? I asked.

Ollie passed away several years ago. Ashley decided to bury him here rather than in Truway since he spent most of his time on the ranch with Sam. When we can't find Sam, we go out to Ollie's grave and there Sam will be, just standing beside it mourning the loss of his friend.

"No, I checked his stall first and it looks like he didn't even eat his breakfast. Since I needed to come talk to you about the investigation, I thought I'd check on Sam's whereabouts, too," Cara replied.

"Well, he's probably saying 'hello' to Ollie before heading down to the campground. You'll find him. Now tell me what you learned from the sheriff," I said with what I hoped sounded like confidence in my voice.

Sam was over fifty years old and moving slower these days. It would break all of our hearts if he'd left us.

"Sheriff Tomes said he'd send some deputies out to scour the surrounding areas including the cave where we found the remains of Grandma Betsy. We still have that boot you sent to have tested for prints several years back. Maybe the boot belongs to our thief. Of course, we won't really know that unless we capture him and check his shoe size," Cara laughed.

It was always a blessing to hear Cara's laugh. She could remain calm and patient in matters like this. She keeps us sane. I'd never heard her refer to Betsy Grace as "Grandma Betsy" before. I liked it.

Cara continued, "We did find a footprint, but it looks like some type of moccasin rather than a boot print, but it's appears to be the same size as the boot. That's why I'm curious about whether he's the owner of the boot or not."

"A moccasin print makes sense. That would explain why we've had trouble in the past finding footprints around the dining hall. How did you find it today? We've not had any rain to speak of in quite some time," I inquired.

"Charlie Jay watered the flowers he planted under one of the dining hall windows so the ground was moist enough for the moccasin print to be visible," she replied.

"That's promising. I predict we'll find our culprit soon. I'll let you know if Sam shows up when you come back later today. I know you have lots to do to prepare for the evening performances," I said.

"Thanks so much for always being here to listen. Your faith in us goes a long way. I don't know what we'd do without you," Cara sighed as she reached down to hug my neck and kiss me on the cheek before walking toward Ollie's grave.

Cara returned shortly after she left with tears streaming down her face. She found Sam lying beside his best buddy's resting place. He would never nod his head and bray a 'good morning' to us ever again. We dug a grave beside Ollie's for him. His cross we made said:

*"In loving memory of
Sam, the snow-white burro,
1956-2007"*

* * *

Juan came to get me later that evening so that I could watch the festivities of the Victory Bound Extravaganza. It would be a bitter sweet time since we laid Sam to rest this morning.

"Are you ready to go see the campers and families for the end of the summer gala?" he asked.

"Sure, but I think it's time we buy you a new truck. This one rides like a stagecoach. I feel every bump on the road. No more long trips in this jalopy and that means even our trips to Whistle Stop Cafe," I snorted.

"Yes ma'am. Glen and I are already looking at buying a new ranch vehicle. What color do you want?" He smiled.

"Red, so I can see you coming up to the house hoping for a trip to the cafe for Joe's special tacos. Do you remember that old blue truck you drove around in the forty's? You continued to drive it even when you only had one headlight," I replied.

When Juan escorted me to the front row, I was in time to hear Charlie Jay award the first group who brought back his note which said, "The bearer of this note will receive $50 dollars which he/she will share with his/her orienteering teammates."

We all clapped and cheered for Carson's group. Charlie Jay continued, "We have another announcement for all of our campers and their families so we would like to ask Carson to remain on stage for this exciting news. As of today, Carson Sanders will be the new Victory Bound Camp Director. Congratulations, Carson!"

The campers started hollering, "Speech. Speech." Carson smiled and said, "Thanks for the honor of serving the people who make this campground what it is. I'm thrilled to lead us for the next 25 years or more. Before I leave the stage, I'd like to ask you to help me applaud the founders of Victory Bound— Cara, Glen, and Aunt Thelma."

Cara helped me up so that I could turn around and face the crowd with her and Glen as we basked in their appreciation.

After the applause died down, Carson invited Cara and Ashley to come up on stage. When they walked up, some of the counselors and campers joined them for the last performance of the evening,

Ashley began singing Betsy Grace's hit song, *Southern Grit & Glamour*. The others harmonized with her. One of the counselors played a guitar while a camper played his violin. I sat in amazement as I listened to this song that would always conjure up thoughts from earlier days of another group who sang this same song on a festival stage in Truway, Texas.

* * *

I can't believe that it's the year 2015. Next year Lottie will be 100 years old. Cara is here around the clock to take care of my needs. I am in a wheel chair now. My hip keeps giving me problems, but I greet each day with enthusiasm that I've lived yet another day.

"Aunt Thelma, do you want to come back into the house. It's a little too chilly out here on the porch, don't you think?" Cara asked.

"No, I have my shawl wrapped around me. I'd like to spend more time talking with God and thanking Him for all of my blessings and thinking about those blessings. I was remembering the day Sam brought you home on his back when you were around ten or so. Do you remember him saving you from your fall on the cacti bed?" I asked.

"I'll never forget that day. It took you two hours to pull all of the quills out of my backside," Cara laughed. She stopped and peered toward the barn as if expecting Sam to come out the door and trot over to say, "Good morning" with his special nod of the head.

* * *

Even though it's almost June, 2015, the mornings are still crisp. There's a lot of excitement in the air as we approach another summer of the Victory Bound Campground. Carson Sanders came by yesterday to tell me news about a famous basketball player, Isaiah Austin, who was destined to play for a professional team and found out five days before the draft that he had Marfans and would be unable to play.

His heart was affected and he was told he may never play basketball competitively again. He turned his sad news into good news by going around the country and sharing his story with others in the hope of raising awareness and funds for Marfans research.

Carson has been an outstanding director and I know he will make the most of Isaiah Austin's visit.

"Thelma, I can't believe that Isaiah Austin has agreed to be our kick-off motivational speaker this year. He's an amazing young man who is so inspirational to hear. We are so fortunate to have him on our team this summer." Carson shared.

Isaiah would not only be here for the kick-off, he planned to stay and work with the campers. This would be the best summer yet for Victory Bound.

*　*　*

The first day was exceptional. Everyone was pumped to spend time with Isaiah. He would be one of the orienteering leaders. Charlie Jay told him he could be the one to wait on the groups to return to the starting line, but he insisted on being with a group. They had to draw straws to see who would be led by Isaiah.

Cara wheeled me to my swing on the front porch when we heard Glen and Carson talking in the front yard. Apparently, one of the orienteering groups found another cave when they got off course somehow.

"Glen, I can't believe what they found," Carson said with big eyes.

"I know. It's unbelievable," Glen replied.

"What's going on?" Cara asked.

We'll wait on Charlie Jay to get here so he can tell the story like only Charlie Jay can. The following is his story:

I was with the group who got off course. Carson stayed back at the starting line and waited for the winning team to bring the note from the last checkpoint. One of the campers noticed an opening in some rocks across a ravine we were trying to figure out how to cross.

We scrambled down one side of the ravine and started climbing up the rocks on the other side. I was leading the expedition so I was the one who saw the opening to the cave entrance. There was a ledge outside the "door" so I told the others to wait while I went in to see who or what was inside. I didn't want to encounter another Gila monster like I did the day I broke my leg or a rattlesnake.

When I went in and turned on my flashlight I noticed right away that someone was living here. There were clothes laying on the cave floor and when I scanned the room, I saw cooking supplies that looked very familiar. I went back to the campers and told them what I'd seen. I took our map and checked our compass to see if we knew where we were. I asked Jason, one of our counselors to continue to find the next checkpoint with the campers while I stayed behind with a couple of the campers to inventory what we found. I picked up an old pair of moccasins and took a saucepan. We backtracked to the starting line so that we could show Carson what we found. It's obvious that our long-term thief was living in this cave.

Everyone was quiet for what seemed like eternity when Glen finally spoke up and said, "We'll contact Sheriff Tomes and ask him to go back to the cave with you, Charlie. Maybe the person living there will return and you will be able to apprehend him."

The search team came back with more items from the cave, but were unsuccessful in finding whoever was staying there.

Charlie Jay was sure that the thief would try to get his stuff back, so he decided to rig a volleyball net as a snare to catch him when he showed up. He and Jason, another one of our counselors climbed a tree and pulled part of the net up with them. They somehow rigged it so that the mystery man would be pulled up in the net if he stepped just right on the hidden rungs of the net.

It sounded complicated to me, but they were determined that this would be the year that our culprit would be caught.

* * *

The next morning Glen came into the house before we even made it to the porch. "Guess what? We got him. Charlie and Jet caught the campground thief in their net. He's middle aged it appears under all of the grime on his clothes and face. His hair is long and matted. He wouldn't talk to us at first, but after we gave him some coffee and food, he opened up."

My name is Henry Wise. My grandfather liked to call me Hank when he was still alive. My parents were killed when I was only two years old. I was destined to go to an orphan's home, but my grandfather broke into the foster caregiver's home and took me away. We've lived in two different caves our entire lives and wrestled our way into different places stealing food and supplies. My favorite place is this place. When I think no one is looking, I watch the activities at night and dream about sitting beside the campfires that you have. I knew you'd eventually catch me. Maybe I wanted to be caught. I guess you'll call the cops and have me arrested now.

"Bring him here," I said.

"Why, Aunt Thelma. He's dirty and stinks. Why would you want him here?" Glen asked.

"He needs a bath before Sheriff Tomes gets here. There's a shower in the back room of the barn. Take him there and clean him up then bring him to the house so Cara can cut his hair. Don't you have some clothes you could put on him, Glen?" I asked.

"Yes, I can give him some clothes. I'll take him to the barn and then bring him to the house if that's what you want me to do," Glen said, and then turned and walked out the door with heavy steps despite his obvious confusion.

After Hank got his bath and changed his filthy clothes, Cara brought a chair out to the front porch so that she could attempt to cut his hair.

While she was cutting away the matted parts he began to tell us about his grandfather.

"Gramps was the best. He knew how to catch most anything for our meals, but sometimes we had to go places and steal things in order to survive," he said.

"Do you remember when you left the first cave you lived in?" I asked.

"No, I never really lived in the first cave Gramps lived in. I do remember the stories he told about a Gila monster that showed up and scared the living daylights out of him," Hank replied.

"What other stories did he tell you about when he lived in the cave in No Man's Gulch?" I asked.

"Well, lots of stories. He told me about a pack of coyotes that he had to scare off once. And there was a cougar that he woke up to sniffing him like he was Sunday dinner. He told me that back in the forties he heard a man and woman fighting up on the ledge. The woman somehow fell either with a push or a stumble. When she landed at the bottom, she hit her head on a rock and died instantly," he told us and then stopped talking because tears were streaming down my face as I heard how my sister died in 1943. It had to be Betsy Grace.

He said his grandfather took her into his cave and buried her there. He also told us he heard a car or truck start up, he thought, before she fell. Hank's grandfather gathered his belongings and moved out of the cave afraid he'd get blamed if someone found the body. When we showed him the ancient boot, Hank nodded and said, "Looks like Gramps."

When Sheriff Tomes came to get Hank I met him on the porch.

"Good morning, Thelma. I appreciate what you did for Hank, but now it's time for me to take him into town. We'll wait for the county judge to return from his vacation before sending the scoundrel to prison," he sighed.

For some reason my heart ached when I thought of Hank going to prison. He was only stealing from us to stay alive and what's worse than that was that the circumstances were not of his making.

"Sherriff, I am not going to press charges. I think it will work out better for Hank to stay on at the ranch. He can live in the room attached to the barn and work to pay off his debts to us," I replied.

"Thelma, you certainly will have a crown waiting for you when you get to heaven," he said as he turned and went back to his car. Besides, because of Hank's testimony we know that Betsy Grace was with someone else before she fell or was pushed and I think I know who that someone was. Wait until Lottie hears this!

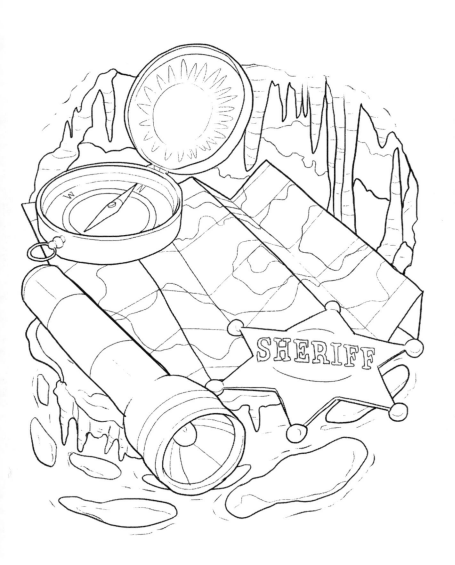

Chapter 11
Thyme Makes a Difference
(Lottie, 2016)

"When I wake up in the morning
and I think about my day,
help me to remember it's all about your way."
Lyrics from It's Your Day, Lord

Every new day is a blessing. I moved into the Sunshine Home a few months back when CJ, Austin, and Ashley sat me down and convinced me it was time to live in an assisted living facility. CJ initially wanted to stay with me and take care of my needs, but I told her she had to help Austin and Ashley with their businesses. She works long hours every day and occasionally sees her old friends Emma Lou and Bea. Emma Lou runs the flower shop and Bea returned from New York where she received a degree in dance from Julliard. She opened Spade's Dance Studio named after one of her instructors and already has a waiting list for classes. I remember a time when Emma Lou told us she thought it was uncanny that Bea became a dance instructor since she and Austin were the ones who slipped and fell into a mud puddle during a three-legged race while all of the kids were in elementary school. CJ and Emma Lou ultimately won that race with their legs tied together. They have all laughed about that day on many occasions.

Bea has a significant person coming in from New York to see the new studio. I hear he's bringing his best friend's son, Sam Taylor with him to show him the sights in Truway. Hopefully, they'll come see me so that I can answer any questions about the days of old if they are so inclined to ask.

I'm still reeling from the shock of hearing about the story Thelma shared about Betsy Grace and her argument with someone on Lost Man's Ledge before she fell or was pushed.

That had to be Tom Frank Buchanan, but he said Betsy Grace never showed up that night. Apparently, he lied. I never trusted that scoundrel even back when he supposedly fell in love with my sister. My thoughts were interrupted by someone knocking on my door.

"Lottie, how are you today?" said Jailee, my favorite nurse at the Sunshine Home. She is Tallulah Belle's great granddaughter and arrived here around the same time I moved.

"I'm thanking the Lord that I woke up once again to embrace this beautiful day. How are you?" I asked.

"I'm just peachy and ready to wheel you down to the parlor. You have guests this morning for breakfast," she smiled.

I knew it was my family. They come early every Saturday morning to eat breakfast with me. We eat eggs, bacon, and pancakes. Pancakes are a treat every weekend.

After breakfast, we enjoy playing dominoes or cards.

"Aunt Lottie, Austin and I are going to Nashville tomorrow. Ashley said she could hold down the fort while we look into the latest news we received from Aunt Thelma." CJ said as we made our way to the activity room.

"Thank you so much, CJ for going back and talking with Tom Frank Buchanan," I sighed.

* * *

CJ and Austin left bright and early the next day. Ashley promised to return today after church with her friends for lunch. I am anxious about the Nashville trip, but excited to meet Bea's fellow and his friend.

"We're here," Ashley said. I raised my head up and looked into those beautiful hazel eyes I knew so well. I must have dozed off while waiting for them to arrive.

"Hi, sweet girl. Who's this other pretty face standing beside you?" I smiled at Bea.

"Hello, Aunt Lottie. It's so good to see you again. I want you to meet my fiancé, Jack Barton, and his best friend's son, Sam Taylor," she motioned toward the handsome men standing beside her.

"Lottie, we've heard great things about you. We want to pick your brain after lunch if that's okay with you," Jack said.

"Sure, it's always fun to work my brain at ninety-nine," I chuckled.

We had roast beef with brown gravy, salad, rolls, and banana pudding for lunch. The young people seemed to enjoy their Sunday dinner. Sam asked, "May I have the honor of pushing your wheel chair into the parlor?" He seemed like a nice young man and very handsome.

"Of course. Thank you," I looked up at him and noticed he was looking at Ashley with admiration written all over his face.

"We've heard that you practically built the town of Truway and wanted to get your advice about something we're interested in pursuing," he said.

When we all got comfortable around the fireplace, Jack took up the conversation. "We want to talk to the local banker about opening a new hospital and clinic here. My degree is in business administration and this smart young man with me has a medical degree. I guess I need to start calling him Dr. Taylor from now on," Jack laughed.

Dr. Thompson died several years ago and his nephew was filling in for him, but I'd heard that he wanted to move into Del Rio and work in a clinic there. We've been waiting on someone who had a desire to settle down in Truway and see to our medical needs.

"I think it's a wonderful idea, but you don't need my advice. Just do it," I told them.

"We wanted your advice because we plan to call it Trinity Hospital in honor of you and your family. What do you think about that idea?" Sam asked.

I could feel my eyes tearing up as I tried to answer him. I choked out, "I'd be honored."

My four visitors left to talk about their plans for their new venture. It's been a long day even though it's barely four o'clock. I think I'll listen to my new audio book for a while before going to bed for the night.

* * *

I opened my eyes to a ringing sound coming from my front room. It was my telephone. Whoever it was must have known that it would take a while for me to answer it because it kept ringing until I finally answered it.

"Hello," I said out of breath.

"Aunt Lottie, it's me. Sorry to bother you so early in the morning, but I had to tell you what we found out." It was CJ and her voice seemed tense.

I took a deep breath and said, "Okay, I'm ready. What did you find out?"

"Tom Frank Buchanan passed away several days ago. We arrived this morning just as they were cleaning out his cell," she said hurriedly.

For a moment, I just stared at the picture of the cross I had on my wall before asking, "Did he say anything to anyone before he died?"

"No, but it's a good thing that we were here because as we were talking with the warden about why we were visiting and asking about his death, one of the guards walked up and handed him an envelope.

The warden glanced at it when his expression changed to one of surprise.

"Mrs. Chilacothe, this letter is addressed to your aunt, but there's no address. It only says, 'Lottie Trinity, Truway, Texas,'" he said.

Before CJ could say another word, I interrupted her and asked, "Have you read the letter yet?"

"No, we called you and knew you'd want to hear it read out loud over the phone unless you want us to wait and read it together in person when we return," CJ said.

"Read it now. The suspense is too much for me to handle and I really want to celebrate my 100th birthday," I replied.

Dear Lottie,

I am writing this letter to you in the hope that the prison warden will find your address and get it to you. The doctor said I need to get my affairs in order before this cancer takes my life. I don't have any family to speak of, and I know that you're not family or even a friend, but I had to tell you again that I didn't hurt Betsy Grace. As I told you when you visited me several years ago, she never showed up to meet me and I didn't wait around to find out why she didn't come.

Looking back on that night, I was angry at her for not being there. I knew she was torn as to what she should do. She loved her daughter so much and her devotion to you and Thelma was something I'd never experienced before in my life.

I remembered something else about that night that I never told you or anyone.

When I was driving to Lost Man's Ledge, I met someone coming from that direction. I couldn't see the driver, but I did notice that it was a blue truck and it only had one headlight piercing through the darkness.

This additional information might not mean much, but I had to tell you about what I saw.

I hope you find the peace that you're searching for concerning Betsy Grace and her death. Unfortunately, I'm going to go to my grave never knowing what happened to her, but I thank the Lord that I had the opportunity to know her. I've asked for His forgiveness and I hope in time you'll find it in your heart to forgive me, too.

Sincerely,

Tom Frank Buchanan

After what seemed like an eternity, CJ sighed heavily into the phone and then said, "Aunt Lottie, are you okay?

"Yes, I'm fine. I don't know what to believe. Please come home so that we can contact Thelma and let her hear what Tom Frank Buchanan wrote before he died," I was able to reply.

Will we ever be able to find out the truth about Betsy Grace's death?

* * *

"Aunt Lottie?" I heard someone saying my name and when I opened my eyes, CJ and Austin were standing in front of me smiling. CJ bent down and hugged me and said, "It's so good to be back here with you. I heard from Jailee that you won bingo three times in a row yesterday. It amazes me how quick your mind is at ninety-nine. Can you believe you will be 100 in three more weeks?"

"Three weeks? Is that all? I hope you're planning a big party. Cara, Glen, and Charlie Jay will be here. If only Thelma was strong enough to come, too, but her hip pain will keep her at home on the ranch, I'm afraid," I said.

"We'll call her when you're ready," CJ smiled again.

"Let's do it right now. I want to hear what she has to say about the letter from Nashville," as I started wheeling my chair down to my room.

"Cara, how are you? I'm so excited to know you will be here in person in a couple of weeks. How is

Aunt Thelma. Is she well enough to talk to Aunt Lottie on the phone?" CJ asked.

"Sure. I will put the phone on speaker so that we can all hear what's being said. Will you do the same?" Cara replied.

CJ put the phone on speaker and I began the conversation, "Thelma, are you there?"

"I'm here, Lottie. How the world are you? You know you have an important birthday just around the corner? I so wish that I could be there in person to celebrate it with you, but I will have to be there in spirit only due to this 'dad burn' hip of mine," Thelma chuckled.

"Thelma, I will miss seeing you. I received a letter from Tom Frank Buchanan that I think you need to hear. CJ and Austin got it from the warden at the prison in Nashville. Unfortunately, they didn't get to see Tom Frank in person. He passed away before they could talk to him," I said.

"What does his letter say? Did he confess to knowing what happened to Betsy?" Thelma asked.

"No, he still maintained that he never got to see her that night, but I want CJ to read it out loud because he added information about that evening we didn't know about," I continued.

CJ read the letter to all within earshot across the phone line between Texas and New Mexico. When she finished, no one said a word.

"Thelma, what do you think about the vehicle that Tom Frank said he met while driving out to Lost Man's Ledge?" I asked.

Again, no one said anything and then I heard Cara say, "Aunt Lottie, something's wrong with Aunt Thelma. I'm afraid this news has upset her for some reason. We're going to hang up, get her a glass of water and her pain medication and call you back later, okay?"

The call that came later was not the one we wanted. Thelma passed away a few hours after we talked to her. My heart is broken into so many pieces! I can't imagine life without Thelma even though she has lived in another state most of our adult lives, she has been with me every day.

Brother Mike showed up almost immediately after we got the call from Cara. CJ must have called him. "Hello, Lottie. I'm here for you, and God is here for you, too."

He didn't say anything further for a while. He sat beside me holding my hand with one of his while wiping the tears from my face with the other.

* * *

Thelma was buried on the Las Bonitas ranch by her husband, Henry. As much as I wanted her buried in the Mount Hope cemetery beside Betsy Grace, I knew she needed to be with her husband. CJ, Austin, and Ashley are still in New Mexico. Brother Mike went with them so that he could perform the funeral service as requested in Thelma's will.

"Lottie?" I lifted my head and saw the man I'd come to love even more in my old age.

"Hello, John Mark. It's good to see you. Can you sit with me for a spell?" I asked.

"Of course. That's why I'm here," he replied.

He sat beside me and reached out to hold my hand, then ever so slowly lifted it up to his worn wrinkled lips and kissed it softly. We sat hand-in-hand until we both fell asleep.

The day before my birthday, CJ and Cara came to see me. Cara said, "Aunt Lottie, I'm so glad I get to be here with you. Aunt Thelma loved you so much. She told me I had to let you know what she discovered about Betsy Grace, but she made me swear I would wait and tell you in person. She didn't let any of you know that her heart was failing. She died of congestive heart failure, but she lived one of the best lives a person could live surrounded by people who loved.

"I miss her so much. What did she tell you about the night Betsy Grace died?" I asked wide-eyed.

"After CJ read the letter from Tom Frank, she asked me to wheel her to her room and send for our ranch foreman, Juan. When Juan came, she asked him to tell her the truth. Had he seen Betsy Grace on the day she died and this is what he said:

Miss Thelma, I'll tell you the truth. I did see her at Lost Man's Ledge before the sun set behind the mountains. I knew she was going to meet that agent from Nashville and leave you and her baby girl. I had to follow her and talk her out of leaving. She started crying and saying I didn't understand anything. She ordered me to go back to the ranch and leave her decisions to her.

I left her standing by the ledge crying as the sun was going down. I drove back to the ranch and as I was driving I met a car headed that direction.

When Betsy didn't come home, I assumed she left and went to Nashville.

I'm sorry I never told you about seeing her. I promise you that she was alive when I left her.

Aunt Thelma closed her eyes and asked Juan to leave her to her thoughts. She never woke up.

Glen and I questioned Juan again and asked him how Aunt Thelma knew about him meeting Betsy that evening. He told us it was the description of his blue truck with only one headlight working. Aunt Thelma remembered his truck and knew it had to be the one that Tom Frank described.

Could Betsy have just plummeted over the edge with no one else around other than Hank's grandfather at the bottom? That's what had to have happened. She must have fallen backwards, blinded by tears of frustration after meeting with Juan. According to her letter to Thelma, she made the right decision to stay with her family and give up the dream for musical fame. In the end it was Thelma who solved the case. It's time to let Betsy Grace rest in peace.

* * *

Today is my 100th birthday. Everyone I know in Truway showed up to bring me cards and presents. Ashley is literally staying in my room in her own hospital bed. She had an appendicitis attack while on a date with Sam, the doctor. He asked her to marry him and before she could respond, she was bending over in agony. It's a good thing he's a doctor or he might think she just didn't want to marry him. He got her to the emergency room before her appendix ruptured. She didn't want to miss my birthday so she talked Sam into giving the order to transfer her here until she's released to go home.

What a day! If I don't wake up tomorrow morning, I will be blessed to go to heaven where I will be surrounded by Mama, Daddy, Betsy Grace, Thelma, and Jean.

Cara is asleep on my bed and CJ is laying on Ashley's bed. The television is on. After a brief commercial about Chilacothe Farms and their new sensation thyme and vegetables in the frozen food section—"Thyme and thyme again, enjoy Chilacothe Farm's vegetables!"

"CJ, you wrote that slogan when you were ten years old, but if my memory serves me right, you won third place and didn't get the opportunity to make a commercial with your slogan. Only the first place winner got that honor," I said.

"Well, it helps to be married to a Chilacothe. Austin found the slogan in a scrapbook of mine and insisted we put it on the TV," she laughed.

We both chuckled, but stopped when we heard Harmony Baker singing, 'It's Your Day, Lord' at the national song festival hosted by Baker's Beats in Nashville.

Ashley found the song in another secret compartment in Betsy Grace's dresser a few months back. We sent it to Harmony and asked her to sing it at the festival.

It's you day, Lord. It's your day. Hear us pray, Lord. Hear us pray. When I wake up in the morning and think about my day, help me to remember, it's all about your way.

When I take that first step forward, remind me what to say. Remind me that it's your day and all about your way.

It's your day, Lord. It's your day. Hear us pray, Lord. Hear us pray.

We heard the announcer say at the end of her song, "That is '*It's Your Day, Lord*' sung by Harmony Baker and written by the late Betsy Grace Trinity Nelson, lead singer of the band, Southern Grit and Glamour!

I closed my eyes and thanked God for my blessings.

Epilogue

September 4, 2016

Dear Cara,

It was so great to see you this summer. I'm excited about seeing you again at Christmas. Ashley and Sam plan to be married on Christmas Eve, but said they wouldn't go on their honeymoon until after Christmas Day so we can spend it together.

Life is busy, but good. Chilacothe Farms is thriving and everyone is doing well. We are blessed!

Aunt Lottie sends her love. I look forward to hearing what's going on in New Mexico. Eat a Jean's Delight taco at the Whistle Stop Cafe for me. Thank you for being the best twin sister a girl could have!

Love that never fails,

CJ

September 11, 2016

Dearest CJ,

I treasure your letters. It's so wonderful to go to the mailbox and see your handwriting on an envelope. Email is great, but nothing beats a handwritten letter.

We're counting the days until Christmas when we'll all be together again witnessing the beautiful union between Ashley and Sam.

Guess what? Glen surprised me with a very unique gift yesterday. I guess I should reference them as two gifts. One appeared between his legs and the other on his left side. Their names are Tuck and Jess and they are miniature burros. I call them my little burritos. Tuck is almost solid white with a brown ring around his left eye. Jess is mostly gray but has four white feet and a white patch on her back. They won't be able to take Sam, the snow-white burro's place in my heart, but I'm sure they will carve out their own space.

I can hardly wait for all of you to visit next summer so I can show them to you. I have enclosed pictures for you to see. I ate a Jean's Delight for you and it was delicious. Kiss Aunt Lottie for me.

Love you forever, Cara

P.S. Tell Ashley that I never told her how happy I am that she met another Sam. It was just meant to be!

Southern Grit & Glamour
Thymeline

1915	Betsy Grace– Born June 26, 1915
	Lottie– Born August 11, 1916
	Thelma– Born November 1, 1918
1933	Southern Grit & Glamour Musical Group is introduced–1933
	Lottie falls in love with John Mark Chilocothe–Summer 1931, but loses him to Geraldine Nelson
	Betsy Grace marries Tommy Earl Nelson–August 13, 1931
1934	Jean Loutes is born–June 5, 1935 [Marries Joe Smallwood–1955]
	Tommy Earl dies– June 15, 1938
1938	
1941	Thelma and Henry marry–October 1, 1941
	Henry dies in WWII–January 6, 1943
	Betsy Grace meets Tom Frank Buchannan–May 10, 1940
	Betsy Grace disappears–January 15, 1943
1956	CJ and Cara born–October 9, 1956
	Lottie owns Big Southern Hair & Highlights, Jean and Joe's Place, and The Flower Shop–1982
	CJ marries Austin Chilocothe–June 5, 1982
	Victory Bound Campground begins–Summer 1982
1982	CJ gets Ollie– Summer 1982
	Ashley Trinity Chilocothe born–March 16, 1983
	Ollie and Sam meet– Summer 1993
	Tom Frank writes his last letter to Lottie
1997	Betsy Grace's remains found–June 1, 1997
	Sam disappears– Summer 2007
	Lottie celebrates her 100th Birthday– August 11, 2016
2016	Thelma's memory of Juan's blue truck, 2016
	Thelma dies–July 28, 2016

1918–2016

189